"You Dance Like You Make Love."

Franco whispered the words into Stacy's ear, and shock made her stumble. Could the man read minds? He caught her quickly, pulling her flush against him. The contact was too intense, too arousing. She jerked back, her gaze slamming into his. Suddenly the air seemed loaded with sexual tension.

Franco moved closer, his hand curving around her waist and his hips punctuating the beat in a purely sensual dance. A mating dance. Not graphic or crude. Just devastatingly, pulse-acceleratingly sensuous.

His gaze never strayed. His eyes had remained locked on hers with an intensity burning in the blue depths that made her feel incredibly attractive and, yes, very desirable.

P9-APJ-159

Dear Reader,

What could possibly be more delicious than a sexy, French chocolatier? I had more fun writing Franco Constantine than I have had with any hero in a very long time. Franco is a true sensualist—a man who believes he knows what he wants and how to get it. I am so glad Stacy Reeves came along to show him the error of his thinking.☺

Throw in a vicarious vacation in magical Monaco and writing this story was an absolute pleasure. I've been fascinated with Monaco since my high school days when I begged my parents to allow me to go to Amherst College in Massachusetts, the alma mater of Prince Albert of Monaco. I was convinced I could make him my prince if only I could meet him. Fate had other plans. I attended college near home, but I did indeed meet my prince.

Happy reading!

Emilie Rose

P.S. Don't miss the next installment of my MONTE CARLO AFFAIRS series—*The Prince's Ultimate Deception* hits store shelves July 2007.

EMILIE ROSE

THE MILLIONAIRE'S INDECENT PROPOSAL

Published by Silhouette Books

America's Publisher of Contemporary Romance

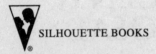

SILHOUETTE BOOKS

ISBN-13: 978-0-373-76804-2
ISBN-10:   0-373-76804-4

THE MILLIONAIRE'S INDECENT PROPOSAL

Copyright © 2007 by Emilie Rose Cunningham

Visit Silhouette Books at www.eHarlequin.com

Printed in U.S.A.

Recent Books by Emilie Rose

Silhouette Desire

Forbidden Passion #1624
Breathless Passion #1635
Scandalous Passion #1660
Condition of Marriage #1675
Paying the Playboy's Price #1732
Exposing the Executive's Secrets #1738
Bending to the Bachelor's Will #1744
Forbidden Merger #1753
The Millionaire's Indecent Proposal #1804

EMILIE ROSE

lives in North Carolina with her college sweetheart husband and four sons. Writing is Emilie's third (and hopefully her last) career. She managed a medical office and ran a home day care, neither of which offers half as much satisfaction as plotting happy endings. Her hobbies include quilting, gardening and cooking (especially cheesecake). Her favorite TV shows include *ER*, *CSI* and Discovery Channel's medical programs. Emilie's a country music fan because she can find an entire book in almost any song.

Letters can be mailed to:
Emilie Rose
P.O. Box 20145
Raleigh, NC 27619
E-mail: EmilieRoseC@aol.com

Bron, Juliet, Sally and Wanda,
you know this book would not have happened without
you. Thanks, ladies, for keeping me on the road.

MJ, thanks for the spark that gave me Franco.

Prologue

"Must you marry every woman you sleep with?" Franco Constantine demanded of his father. Furious, he paced the salon of the family chateau outside Avignon, France. "This one is younger than me."

His father shrugged and smiled—the smile of a besotted old fool. "I'm in love."

"No, Papa, you're in lust. Again. We cannot afford another one of your expensive divorce settlements. Our cash reserves are tied up in expanding Midas Chocolates. For God's sake, if you refuse to have a prenuptial agreement, then at least sign everything over to me before you marry her and jeopardize our business and the family properties with mistake number five."

Armand shook his head. "Angeline is not a mistake. She is a blessing."

Franco had met the misnamed harpy at lunch. She was no angel. But he knew from past experience his father would not listen when a woman had him transfixed. "I disagree."

Armand rested a hand on Franco's shoulder. "I hate to see you so bitter, Franco. Granted, your ex-wife was a selfish bitch, but not all women are."

"You're wrong. Women are duplicitous and mercenary creatures. There is nothing I want from one that I cannot buy."

"If you'd stop dating spoiled rich women and find someone with traditional values like Angeline, you'd find a woman who would love you for yourself and not your money."

"Wrong. And if your paramour loves you and not your wealth, she'll stick by you once you've divested yourself, and I won't have to borrow against our estate *again,* close stores or lay off workers when your ardor cools and her lawyers start circling."

"If you want to control the Constantine holdings so badly, then marry."

"I won't endanger the family assets by marrying again."

"And what of an heir? Someone to inherit all this when you and I are gone?" Armand's sweeping gesture encompassed the chateau which had been in the family for hundreds of years.

Something in his father's tone raised the hackles on the back of Franco's neck. "Is Angeline pregnant?"

"No. But son, you are thirty-eight. I should be bouncing grandbabies on my knee by now. Since you're not willing to provide heirs to our estate then I think perhaps I should. Angeline is only thirty. I could have several more sons and daughters by her before I die."

"You can't be serious. You're seventy-five."

His father speared him with a hard glance. "If you marry before my September wedding, I'll sign everything over to you. If you do not…" He extended his arms and shrugged. "I'll take matters into my own hands."

Franco could easily find a woman to marry. Any number of his acquaintances would agree, but the stench of his ex-wife's betrayal still clung to him. He'd been a young love-struck fool, blind to Lisette's faults and her treachery. He would never let a woman dupe him like that again. Marriage was out of the question.

He stood toe to toe with his father. "If I find one of these mythical paragons and prove she's just as greedy as the rest of her sex, then you will sign the Constantine properties over to me without a parody of a marriage on my part."

"Prove it how exactly?"

How indeed? "I'll offer her a million euros for the use of her body for one month without the pretense of love or the possibility of marriage. That amount is but a fraction of what each of your divorces has cost us."

"I accept your terms, but don't try to weasel out of this by finding an impossible woman. She must be one who you find attractive and beddable, and who you would be willing to marry if she cannot be bought."

A woman who could not be bought. No such animal existed.

Confident he would win, Franco extended his hand to shake on the deal. Victory would not only be sweet, it would be easy, and his father's most recent parasite would not get the chance to sink her fangs in the family coffers and suck them dry.

One

"*Le chocolat qui vaut son poids en or,*" Stacy Reeves read the gilt script on the shop window aloud. "What does that mean?" she asked her friend Candace without looking away from the mouthwatering display of chocolates on gold-rimmed plates.

"Chocolate worth its weight in gold," a slightly accented and thoroughly masculine voice replied. Definitely not Candace.

Surprised, Stacy pivoted on her sandaled foot. Wow. Forget chocolate. The dark-haired blue-eyed hunk in front of her looked good enough to eat.

"Would you care for a piece, mademoiselle? My treat." Monsieur Gorgeous indicated the shop door with his hand. A silver-toned, wafer-thin watch winked beneath his suit sleeve. Platinum, she'd bet, from the affluent look of what had to be a custom-tailored suit.

Nothing from a department store would fit those broad shoulders, narrow hips and long legs so perfectly.

Never mind that she'd probably dream of licking chocolate from the deep cleft in his chin tonight, Stacy had learned the hard way that when something looked too good to be true it was. Always. A seductively sexy stranger offering free gourmet chocolate had to be a set-up because sophisticated guys like him didn't go for practical accountants like her. And her simple lilac sundress and sensible walking sandals weren't the stuff of which male fantasies were made.

She glanced up and down the Boulevard des Moulins, one of the principality of Monaco's shopping streets, searching for her friend. Candace was nowhere in sight, but she had to be behind Mr. Delectable's appearance and offer. Her friend had joked about finding husbands for each of her bridesmaids before her wedding in four weeks time. At least Stacy had thought she was joking. Until now.

Stacy tilted her head, considered the man in question and gave him a saccharine smile. "Does that line usually work for you with American tourists?"

The corners of his oh-so-tempting lips twitched and his eyes glinted with humor beneath thick, straight eyebrows. He pressed a ringless left hand to his chest. "You wound me, mademoiselle."

With his fantasy good looks he had to have an epic ego to match. "I sincerely doubt it."

She scanned the sidewalks again looking for her MIA friend. Anything would be better than embarrassing herself by drooling over something she couldn't have. Namely *him* or the five-dollar—make that euro—per-piece candy.

"You are looking for someone? A lover, perhaps?"

Lover. Just hearing him say the word, rolling that *R,* gave her goose bumps.

"A friend." One who'd been right behind her seconds ago. Candace must have ducked into one of the quaint shops nearby, either to purchase something wedding-related or to spy if she was the one responsible for this encounter. After all, stopping by the chocolate shop had been Candace's idea.

"May I assist you in locating your friend?"

He had the most amazing voice. Deep and velvety. Was the accent French or native Monégasque? Stacy could listen to him talk for hours.

No. She couldn't. She was here with Candace, the bride-to-be, and two other bridesmaids to help prepare for Candace's wedding the first weekend in July, not to have a vacation romance.

"Thanks, but no thanks." Before Stacy could walk away, Candace popped out of the shop next door waving a scrap of lace.

"Stacy, I found the most exquisitely embroi-dered…" She trailed off as she spotted the Adonis beside Stacy. Surprise arched her pale eyebrows. "…handkerchief."

Maybe this wasn't a set-up. Stacy rocked back on her heels, folded her arms and waited for the inevitable. Candace had naturally white-blond hair and big baby-blue eyes. Her innocent Alice-in-Wonderland looks tended to bowl men over. No doubt this guy would fall at Candace's dainty feet. Stacy had never had that problem and that suited her fine. *Forever* wasn't in the cards for her. She'd never trust a man that much.

"Mademoiselle." Tall, Dark and Tempting bowed slightly. "I am trying to convince *vôtre amie* to allow me to gift to her *un chocolat,* but she questions my inten-tions. Perhaps if I buy you both lunch she will see that I'm quite harmless."

Harmless? Ha! He radiated smooth charm in the way that only a European man could.

A cunning smile curved Candace's lips and her eyes narrowed on Stacy. Uh-oh. Stacy stiffened. Whenever she saw that expression, someone was getting ready to try and pull a fast one on the IRS, and that meant trouble for Stacy, their accountant. "I'm sorry, Monsieur…? I didn't catch your name."

He offered his hand. "Constantine. Franco Constantine."

Recognition sparked in Candace's eyes, but the name meant nothing to Stacy. "I've been looking forward to meeting you, Monsieur Constantine. My fiancé, Vincent Reynard, has spoken of you often. I'm Candace Meyers, and this is my one of my bridesmaids, Stacy Reeves."

Mr. Wonderful's considerable charms shone back on Stacy with the heat of the noonday sun. He offered his hand. Darn protocol. She'd been warned during the hours-long etiquette session delivered by Candace's soon-to-be sister-in-law that the inhabitants of this tiny country were quite formal and polite. Refusing to shake his hand would be an insult.

Franco's fingers closed around Stacy's. Warm. Firm. Lingering. His charisma spread over Stacy like butter on hot bread. *"Enchanté, mademoiselle."*

She snatched her hand free and blamed the spark skipping up her arm on static electricity caused by the warm, dry climate. A predatory gleam flashed in his eyes, and warning prickles marched down Stacy's spine. Dangerous.

He turned back to Candace. "May I offer my congratulations on your upcoming nuptials, Mademoiselle Meyers? Vincent is a lucky man."

"Thank you, monsieur, and I would love to accept

your luncheon invitation, but I'm afraid I'll have to decline. I have a meeting with the caterer in an hour. Stacy, however, is free for the rest of the afternoon."

Stacy's jaw dropped. She snapped it closed and glared at her friend. Embarrassment burned her cheeks. "I am not. I'm here to help you plan your wedding. *Remember?*"

"Madeline, Amelia and I have everything under control. You have a nice lunch. We'll catch up with you tonight before we go to the casino. Oh, and monsieur, the hotel has already received your RSVP to the wedding and the rehearsal dinner. Merci. Au revoir." Candace waggled her fingers and departed.

Stacy considered murder. But she'd read that Monaco had a truly impressive police force. There was no way she could get away with strangling the petite blonde in broad daylight on a crowded street, and rotting away in a European prison wasn't exactly the financially secure future she had planned for herself.

A plan now in jeopardy.

Worry immediately weighted her shoulders, but she slammed the barriers in place. *Stop it. This is Candace's month. Don't ruin it for her.*

But Stacy wasn't the type to hide her head in the sand. She knew she had some difficult days ahead. *Not now. You have a more urgent problem standing in front of you.* She blinked away her distressing thoughts and examined the man problem. She hadn't missed Candace's not-so-subtle hint that Franco Constantine was close enough to the Reynards to have been invited to the intimate rehearsal dinner for only a dozen or so guests.

In other words, *play nice.*

Franco grasped Stacy's bare elbow as if he knew making a fast escape topped her to-do list. She felt those long fingers clear down to her toes, and it rattled her that an impersonal touch from a stranger could wreak havoc on her metabolism.

"If you will give me but a moment, Mademoiselle Reeves, I must speak to the shopkeeper, and then I am at your disposal."

He escorted Stacy inside the chocolate shop. The heavenly aroma was enough to give her a willpower-melting sugar rush. After greeting the clerk, Franco commenced a conversation in rapid-fire French…or something that sounded like French.

Stacy shamelessly eavesdropped while perusing the offerings in the glass cases, but she only managed to translate every tenth word or so. Despite the money-back guarantee on the box of *Speak French in 30 Days* CDs she had listened to during the month prior to leaving Charlotte, North Carolina, she wasn't prepared for natives speaking the language at Grand Prix speed.

She caught a hint of crisp, citrus cologne and the hair on the back of her neck rose. Without looking over her shoulder she knew Franco stood immediately behind her. After bracing herself against his potent virility, she turned.

"Mademoiselle?" He held a sinful morsel aloft. What else could she do but take a bite? Her teeth sank into dark chocolate and a tart cherry. Her eyes closed and she fought a moan as she chewed. Ohmigod. Yum. Yum. *Yum.*

Cherry juice dribbled on her chin, but before she could wipe it away Franco's thumb caught it and pressed it between her lips. Knowing she shouldn't, but unable to think of a way to avoid it, Stacy swallowed and then darted out her tongue. The taste of blatantly sexy male combined with the most decadently rich chocolate she'd ever sampled slammed her with sexual arousal like nothing she'd ever experienced.

She dragged a sobering breath through her nose and

struggled to fortify her quaking ramparts. Before she could make her excuses and bolt, Franco lifted the second half of the candy to her mouth. She tried to evade his touch, but his thumb grazed her bottom lip, and then, holding her gaze, he lifted the digit to his mouth and licked the remaining confection from his skin with one slow swipe.

Her pulse stuttered. *Gulp.* Seduction in a suit. The chocolate hit her stomach like a wrecking ball, and the desire in Franco's eyes rolled over her like a heat wave, intensifying the disturbing reactions clamoring inside her.

"Shall we dine, mademoiselle?" He offered his arm in a courtly gesture.

There was no way she could go to lunch with him. Franco Constantine was too…too…too *everything*. Too attractive. Too confident. And judging by his apparel, too rich for her. She couldn't afford to become involved with such a powerful man. If she did, she could very well repeat her mother's mistakes and spend the rest of her life paying for it.

She backed toward the exit. "I'm sorry. I just remembered I have a…a dress fitting."

She yanked open the shop's glass door and fled.

Stacy slammed into the luxurious four-bedroom penthouse suite she shared with Candace, Amelia and Madeline at the five-star Hôtel Reynard. There were perks in having a friend marrying the hotel chain owner's son.

All three women looked up from the sitting area.

"Why are you back so soon?" Candace asked.

"Why did you throw me at that man?" Stacy fumed.

Candace tsked. "Stacy, what am I going to do with you? Franco is perfect for you, and the sparks between the two of you nearly set the shop's awning on fire. You should have had lunch with him. Do you know who he is? His family owns Midas Chocolates."

"The shop?"

"The globally famous company. Godiva's number-one competitor. We have a store in Charlotte. Franco's the CEO of the whole shebang and one of Vincent's best friends. He happens to be absolutely yummy."

No argument there. "I'm not looking for a vacation fling."

Madeline, a nurse in her early thirties, swept her long, dark curls off her face. "Then let me have him. From Candace's description before you arrived Franco sounds beyond sexy. A short, intense affair with no messy endings sounds perfect, and I won't have to worry about getting dumped because we'll be leaving after the wedding anyway."

A vacation affair. Stacy couldn't imagine ever being so nonchalant about intimacy. Intimacy made her feel vulnerable which is probably why she avoided it 99 percent of the time. In her nomadic life she'd never had a friendship that lasted more than a few months until she and Candace had bonded over an IRS audit three years ago when the large accounting firm Stacy worked for had assigned her to Candace's case. Having a friend was a new experience—one Stacy liked—even if she did sometimes feel like an outsider with this trio of hospital workers. Madeline and Amelia were Candace's friends, but Stacy hoped they'd be hers too by the time they left Monaco. Otherwise, if Candace moved away after the wedding Stacy would have no one. Again.

But the idea of Madeline with Franco made Stacy uneasy, which was absolutely ridiculous considering she'd spent less than ten minutes in the man's company, and she had no claim on him. Nor did she want one. Could she have a vacation romance? No. Absolutely not. It just wasn't in her cautious makeup.

"So, is he sexy?" asked Amelia, the starry-eyed romantic of the group.

The women's expressions told Stacy they expected some kind of response. But what? She knew nothing about girl talk. "Yes. B-but in a dangerous way."

"Dangerous?" the three parroted in unison, and then Candace asked, "How so? Franco seemed perfectly civilized to me and very polite."

None of these women knew about Stacy's childhood. And she didn't want to share the shameful details. Not now. Not ever. From the time Stacy was eight years old she'd known she and her mother were running from something every time they packed up—or not—and moved to a new city. Stacy hadn't figured out from what or whom until it was too late.

She swallowed the nausea rising in her throat. "Franco Constantine exudes power and money. If things went wrong between you, he could afford to track you down no matter how far you ran."

The women looked as if her answer made no sense to them. But it made perfect sense to Stacy. Her father had been a wealthy man. When he'd abused his wife the authorities had looked the other way, and when she'd run he'd used his resources to track her down. It had taken him eleven years to get even.

Wealthy, powerful men bent the rules to suit their needs, and they considered themselves above the law. Therefore, Stacy did her best to avoid them.

Franco Constantine definitely fell into the Avoid column.

* * *

Franco studied Stacy Reeves from across the casino. She was perfect for his purpose, exactly the type of female his father had described. And he would have her. No matter the cost. With women there was always a cost. The question was, would she be worth it?

Without a doubt.

In all his thirty-eight years he'd never had such an instant visceral reaction to a woman before. Not even to his ex-wife. From the moment he'd caught the reflection of Stacy's expressive eyes in the shop window this morning he had wanted her to look at him the way she looked at the chocolate. Ravenously.

The contrast between her demure dress, the reserve she wore like a cloak and those hungry eyes had intrigued him. The touch of her tongue on his finger had electrified him. If she could arouse him with such a small gesture, then he couldn't wait to experience the results of a more intimate encounter.

A quick call to Vincent had garnered him a few pertinent details about Mademoiselle Reeves and had confirmed that she was suitable for his needs. Yes, playing his father's game would indeed be pleasurable.

Franco ordered two glasses of champagne and made his way toward her. She stood back from the roulette table in the Café de Paris, observing the trio of women she'd come in with, but not participating in the gambling. In fact, she hadn't made a single wager since she'd arrived half an hour ago.

Tonight she'd twisted her shoulder-length chestnut hair up on the back of her head, revealing a pale nape, a slender neck and delicate ears he could not wait to nibble. Her floor-length gown—a sleeveless affair the color of aged ivory—gently outlined her curves but unfortunately covered her remarkable legs. She'd draped a lacy wrap over her shoulders and strapped on high-heeled gold sandals.

Elegant. Subtle. Desirable.

Mais oui. They would be magnificent together. Anticipation quickened his blood as he reached her side. He paused long enough to savor her scent. Gardenias. Sultry, yet sweet. *"Vous êtes très belle ce soir, mademoiselle."*

She startled and turned. "Monsieur Constantine."

"Franco." He offered a flute and ignored her stiff, unwelcoming posture. Her blue-green eyes, as changeable as the Mediterranean, were more azure than they'd been earlier in the day. What color would they be when they made love? He had every intention of finding out.

After a moment's hesitation she accepted the drink. *"Merci, Mon—"*

He covered her fingers with his on the fragile crystal, stilling her words. He wanted to hear his name on her lips. "Franco," he repeated.

Her lips parted and the tip of her tongue glided over her plump cherry-red flesh. He nearly gave in to the need to taste her, but he restrained himself with no small effort. She was skittish. He had to move slowly if he wanted to successfully close this deal.

"Franco." She gave his name the French pronunciation not the nasally American one he'd grown to hate during his graduate studies in the U.S.

He touched the rim of his glass to hers. *"À nous."*

She blinked and frowned. "I'm sorry?"

"To us, Stacy." She hadn't given him leave to use her name, and he was taking liberties—the first of many he intended to take with the alluring American.

Her eyes darkened and rejection stamped her fine features, but her cheeks pinked. "I don't think—"

"Monsieur Constantine," a feminine voice interrupted.

He reluctantly released Stacy's hand, and forcing his lips into a polite smile, turned to the trio of women. *"Bonsoir, mesdemoiselles."*

Vincent's fiancée introduced her friends, and while etiquette decreed Franco greet each lady, every fragment of his being remained focused on the woman who would soon be his lover. He noticed each nervous shift of Stacy's body, heard the sounds of her silk dress sliding over her skin the way his hands soon would, and he relished the catch of her breath as he deliberately brushed against her when he motioned for a waiter. He ordered beverages for each of the women and then held Stacy's gaze as she lifted her flute to her mouth. He mimicked her actions, wishing it were her warm lips against his instead of the cool glass.

The brunette Madeline sidled closer, making her interest known with her direct stare and come-hither stance while the auburn-haired Amelia blushed and looked away from the other woman's bold behavior. Both women were attractive, but he only had eyes for Stacy. Eventually, the trio turned back to the roulette wheel, affording him the privacy with his quarry he craved. Or as much privacy as one could have in a crowded casino.

"Have you wagered?" He knew she hadn't. He'd been watching.

"No."

He reached in his pocket, retrieved a handful of chips and offered them to her. "Try your luck?"

Her mouth opened, closed, opened again. "That's ten thousand doll—euros."

"Oui."

Wide-eyed, she backed away. "No. No, thank you."

"You wish to play for higher stakes? We can go to the Salon Touzeta, if you like."

"That's a private room."

"*Oui.*"

She looked at her friends, as if hoping they'd rescue her, but the wheel held their attention. "I don't gamble."

The more she refused, the more he wanted her. Was she playing hard to get to torment him or to raise her price? Very likely both. But he would win. Since his wife's betrayal he always did. "You owe me the pleasure of your company at a meal."

Wary eyes locked with his. "Why me? Why not someone who's interested and willing?" A slight tilt of her head indicated her brunette companion.

He shrugged. "Who knows why a body sings for one and not the other?"

Her lace wrap slipped from her shoulder. Franco lifted his hand and dragged a knuckle along the exposed skin of her upper arm. Her shiver before she stepped out of reach gratified him. She would be a responsive lover. "Have dinner with me, Stacy."

"I don't think that's a good idea."

"Have dinner with me," he repeated. "If you choose not to see me privately again afterward, then I will accept your decision."

Her chin lifted. "And if I refuse?"

Enjoying her cat-and-mouse game, he smiled. Her breath caught audibly. *Bien.* The attraction wasn't one-sided. "Then you and your friends will be seeing me quite often."

Slightly imperfectly aligned white teeth captured her bottom lip. How had she escaped the American obsession with a perfect smile? "One dinner. That's it?"

"*Oui, mademoiselle.* Because I can take no for an answer when the woman really means it."

Her shoulders squared. "I mean it."

He could not prevent a small smile. "*Non.* Your mouth says one thing, but your beautiful eyes say another. You want to have dinner with me."

Her cheeks flushed and her kissable lips compressed. She nodded sharply. "One dinner and then you leave me alone."

A surge of adrenaline shot through him at the small success. He touched his champagne flute to hers. Victory was within his grasp.

"*À nous,* Stacy. *Nous serons magnifiques ensemble.*"

Two

Nous serons magnifiques ensemble.

"We will be magnificent together." Stacy groaned and tossed her French-to-English-to-French dictionary on the coffee table. Her flushed skin and restlessness had nothing to do with the morning sun streaming through the hotel sitting room's open curtains or her eagerness to get out and see more of Monaco. The blame for her twitchiness could be placed solely on the desire in Franco's eyes last night when he'd said the mysterious phrase before taking his leave.

She'd dreamed about him, about those hungry eyes and that deeply cleft chin. No surprise there, since the man's blatant sexiness was an assault on her senses.

Franco Constantine was pursuing her and she had no idea why. The country was full of more beautiful, more sophisticated and more available women, but for some incomprehensible reason he wanted *her*. And, like it or not, as foolish as it might be—and it was incredibly foolish—she was attracted to him too. Scary, heady stuff. Her instincts told her to blow him off, but his friendship with Vincent made that tricky. Stacy couldn't afford to be rude and risk upsetting Candace.

Stacy shifted uneasily on the sofa. Surely she could manage a meal with him without getting in over her head? One dinner and then he'd promised to leave her alone. She'd eaten with a number of clients who'd implied they wanted her handling more than their books, and she'd resisted easily enough. Of course, she'd never been tempted like this. Franco was beyond her experience, and she couldn't help feeling as if she'd made a deal she would regret.

The door to Madeline's bedroom opened and the brunette shuffled into the sitting area. Her gaze roamed over the coffee carafe Stacy had ordered from room service and Stacy's empty cup. "My God, how long have you been up?"

"A few hours. My body clock is confused."

"So are you and Franco going to hook up?"

Stacy's blouse and pants abraded her suddenly warm flesh. "We're going to have dinner and then he's all yours."

Her skin prickled anew. Why did that bother her? Franco was too rich and powerful for her and far out of her league, but that didn't mean the other woman couldn't enjoy him.

"No thanks. I met someone after you came upstairs last night, and man oh man, is he *hot*." Madeline poured herself a cup of coffee.

This was the girl talk Stacy didn't do so well. Where were the boundaries? What was she supposed to ask? What topics should she avoid? She settled for a non-committal, "Oh?"

"Oh yeah." Madeline smiled as she sipped. "He's going to act as my tour guide after we kill our diets this morning sampling the different wedding cakes the hotel chef has prepared."

Amelia glided silently into the room. "Did I hear you say you're going out today? Me too, if for no other reason than to avoid Toby Haynes."

"Who?" Stacy asked. The name sounded vaguely familiar.

Amelia grimaced. "Toby Haynes, the race-car driver for the NASCAR team Reynard Hotels sponsors. It was a fire in his pit that burned Vincent."

"Speaking of Vincent, I guess you've both met the groom since he was a patient at the hospital where you work?" Stacy hadn't—just one more reason she felt like the outsider in the group. Story of her life.

"Yes and his cocky Casanova driver is here in Monaco and determined to be a pain in my backside," Amelia grumbled.

"Perhaps you and I could do the tourist thing together," Stacy suggested somewhat hesitantly. These women barely knew her and might prefer to spend their time with someone else.

"Sounds great. I'll get dressed." The suite doorbell chimed. Amelia, already on her feet, answered. When she turned around she held a beautiful bouquet of gardenias. "They're for you, Stacy."

Stacy's heart stalled. No one had ever sent her flowers. She accepted the fragrant arrangement, extracted the card and read the slashing black script. Tonight. 20:00. Franco.

"Who are they from?" Amelia asked.

Stacy couldn't find her voice. Were the gardenias a coincidence or had he actually noticed her perfume?

Madeline read the card over Stacy's shoulder. "Her

delicious chocolatier. Monaco operates on military time. He's picking you up tonight at eight. *Bon chance, mon amie.*"

Stacy forced an unsteady smile. She'd need more than luck to resist the sexy Frenchman.

Madeline rose, stretched and yawned. "Amelia, make sure Stacy has something suitably sexy to wear. And Stace, tuck a few condoms in your purse. Be prepared."

Prepared for Franco Constantine? Impossible.

Thanks to Candace and Amelia, Stacy was as prepared as she possibly could be for her evening with temptation in the form of Franco Constantine, minus the condoms which she most definitely would not need.

After sampling enough wedding cakes to send her blood sugar into orbit, she, Candace and Amelia had attempted to walk off the calories by touring La Condamine, the second-oldest section of Monaco, this morning, and then exploring the wonderful shops on the Rue Grimald in the early afternoon. Afterward the women had returned to the hotel and turned Stacy over to the spa staff for a facial, a manicure and a pedicure.

Stacy stood in front of the mirror and smoothed her hands over the gown they'd found in a European designer clothing outlet. Claiming it would be perfect for the rehearsal dinner, Candace had overridden Stacy's polite refusal and insisted on buying it for her. The sapphire fabric skimmed Stacy's figure without clinging, and the halter top gave her enough support that she didn't need a bra. She felt worlds more sophisticated in this gown than in anything she'd ever owned.

The phone rang and Stacy nearly jumped out of her gold sandals. Her suitemates were out. She crossed her bedroom and lifted the receiver. "Hello."

"*Bonsoir,* Stacy," Franco's deep voice rumbled over her. "I am in the lobby. Shall I come up?"

Her pulse fluttered like the flag over the prince's palace in a stiff breeze. Franco in her suite? Absolutely not.

"No. I'll come down." She hung up the phone and pressed a hand over her pounding heart. "One dinner. You can do this."

She draped her lace wrap over her shoulders, grabbed her gold clamshell evening purse and headed out the door. Her stomach stayed behind as the elevator swiftly descended from the penthouse to the lobby level. The doors opened and there he was, a six-foot-something package of irresistible—correction, completely resistible—male. Franco leaned against a marble pillar looking as rich and sinful as the chocolate he'd fed her. Stacy inhaled slowly and then moved forward on less-than-steady legs.

Franco spotted her and straightened. A midnight-blue suit and a shirt in a paler shade emphasized his eyes as his appreciative gaze glided from her upswept hair to her newly polished toenails before returning to her face. Every cell in her body quivered in the wake of the leisurely visual caress. He took her hand and bent over it, brushing his lips against her knuckles in a touch so light she could have imagined it. The whisper of his breath on her skin made her shiver.

He straightened and his intensely blue eyes burned into hers. "*Vous enlevez mon souffle,* Stacy."

There was no way she could translate even the simplest sentences when he looked at her or touched her that way. "I'm sorry?"

"You take my breath away."

"Oh." *Oh? That's it? That's the best you can come up with?* She tugged her hand and after a moment's resistance he released her. "Thank you. And thank you for the flowers. They're lovely. But you shouldn't have."

"I could not resist. Their fragrance reminded me of you." He offered his elbow. Stacy couldn't think of a courteous way to decline. Reluctantly, she threaded her hand through his bent arm and let him escort her from the cool interior of the hotel into the warm evening air. The lights of Monaco twinkled around them in the falling dusk. He paused outside the entrance. "The restaurant is only a few blocks away. Shall we walk? Or would you prefer a taxi?"

"You didn't drive?" She'd pictured him as the powerful-sports-car type, the kind who careened around the hairpin turns at breakneck speed like a Grand Prix driver.

"I drove. My villa is in the hills overlooking Larvotto. Too far to walk. But there is no parking near the restaurant."

She and Candace had taken the bus to Larvotto beach yesterday before she'd met Franco. In a country covering less than one square mile how likely was she to be able to avoid him until the wedding once this obligatory date ended? The odds weren't in her favor. "Let's walk."

A breeze stirred her hair. He caught a stray strand and tucked it behind her ear. The stroke of his finger on the sensitive skin along her jaw made her hormones riot and her pulse leap. "I would like to show you the view of Larvotto from my terrace. *C'est incroyable.*"

No matter how incredible the view she had no intention of seeing it. *Get this date on an impersonal footing.* "How is it that you know Vincent exactly?"

A knowing smile curved his lips, as if he knew she wanted to tread safer ground. He turned and led her down the sidewalk. "We shared an apartment during graduate school."

She frowned up at him. "But didn't Vincent go to MIT?"

"*Oui.*"

"You lived in the States? No wonder your English is so good." They turned the corner and the smell of Greek food from a nearby sidewalk café permeated the air. Her mouth watered and her stomach rumbled, reminding her that she hadn't eaten since the cake overdose this morning.

"Midas Chocolates distributes product on six continents. It pays to be fluent in several languages. Interpreters are not always available or reliable." He turned down a narrow alley she would have missed and stopped in front of a salmon-pink building with a red tiled roof. The only signage was the address in brass script above an unremarkable wooden door. "Here we are."

"This is a restaurant? It looks like a private residence." She'd hoped for something less intimate, like one of the numerous cafés lining the streets. She still couldn't get over how people brought their pets into restaurants. Stacy pulled her arm free on the pretext of adjusting her wrap and instantly missed his body heat even on this sultry night. *Get over it.*

"It is a secret kept by the locals. Good food. Good music. Exceptional company."

She cursed the flush warming her skin. The man issued compliments too easily, and she didn't intend to be swayed by his glib tongue. She'd been burned by insincere flattery once before. The humiliating aftermath wasn't something she wanted to relive.

He opened the door with one hand. The other curved behind her waist, palm splayed. She could feel the imprint through the thin fabric of her dress as he guided her forward. She hurried inside only to stop suddenly in the tiled foyer.

This must have been someone's home once, but now a maître d's stand occupied the niche beneath a curving staircase. The dining rooms Stacy could see to the left and right were furnished with half a dozen widely spaced, candlelit tables draped in white linens. Crystal and silver glinted in the flickering light, and music played quietly in the background. Intimate, but not unbearably so. Some of Stacy's tension eased. She could handle this.

But internal alarm bells rang as the hostess led them upstairs and finally stopped in a small private room with only one table. This very likely had once been a bedroom. Any plans Stacy might have had to keep this meal impersonal by watching the other patrons or trying to translate their conversations evaporated. The same music she'd heard downstairs drifted through exterior doors left open to a wrought-iron railed balcony. A gentle flower-scented breeze stirred the sheer curtains and made the candle flames dance.

Franco seated her. She startled when his fingertips brushed her upper arms, dragging her wrap back so that it bared her shoulders. He draped the lace over her chair, and then sat at a right angle to her, his knee touching hers beneath the table. She shifted away from the contact, but that didn't stop the buzz of awareness vibrating through her.

An older man entered. He and Franco held a rapid-fire discussion Stacy couldn't understand, and then he departed. "Was that French?"

"*Non.* Monégasque, the local dialect. It's a combination of French and Italian."

"Is that what you were speaking at your shop the day we met?"

"*Oui,* but French is the language spoken most often in Monaco. Do you speak French?"

"A little. I had the required two semesters in college and then I listened to some instructional CDs before coming here."

He covered her hand with his on the table and stroked his thumb over the inside of her wrist. Her pulse bolted like a startled rabbit. "You may practice on me, if you wish."

The spark in his eyes said she needn't limit her practice to the language. Stacy pulled her hand free and tangled her fingers in her lap. Looking away, she chewed the inside of her lip and tried to ignore the tension knotting low in her belly.

Their server returned with a tray of tiny stuffed tomatoes and mushrooms, poured the wine and departed even though they hadn't ordered yet.

"There aren't any menus?"

"*Non.* Trust me. You will not be disappointed."

Trust. He couldn't possibly know how difficult it was for her to trust anyone but herself. "What if I have food allergies?"

"Do you?"

"No," she admitted, feeling slightly ashamed for being difficult. She sipped her wine, sampled a crab-stuffed tomato and struggled to find a topic that would dilute the romantic atmosphere. "I was surprised to discover that Monaco relies heavily on French laws, including the French wedding ceremony and that they've removed the promise of fidelity from their vows. Why is that? Can French men not be faithful?"

Franco sat back, the smile slipping from his face. "I was faithful to my wife."

That doused the warmth in her belly. "You're married?"

"Divorced." And bitter by the sounds of that one bitten-off word. "You?"

"I've never been married." She'd never even been in

a long-term relationship. She'd had one clumsy encounter in high school and a brief intimate relationship with a guy from work. She shoved the bad memories back into their cave. "How long were you married?"

"Five years."

"What happened?" None of her business really, but she'd never met a divorcé who didn't want to talk about the unpleasant experience, and dull as it may be, hearing about someone else's dirty laundry was better than having Franco focus his seductive charms on her.

He shrugged, but the movement seemed stiff instead of casual. "We wanted different things."

"Do you have any children?"

"Non."

Had she imagined his hesitation? "Do you keep in touch?"

"I have not seen Lisette since the divorce."

"And you're okay with that?"

"Absolument."

Absolutely. She studied Franco, trying to gauge his sincerity. His direct gaze showed no doubts, no prevarications.

Her father hadn't willingly let go. Had that been because he'd loved her mother so much or because he'd considered her a possession, as the therapists had said? Stacy shook off the questions to which she'd never have answers and focused on her date. "Have you always lived in Monaco?"

"Non. I grew up outside Avignon, France. My family home is still there. I relocated my residence and Midas Chocolates headquarters here eight years ago after my divorce." His expression turned speculative. "You are trying very hard not to enjoy our evening, Stacy. Why is that?"

He read her too easily. "You're mistaken."

"Then prove me wrong by dancing with me."

When he put it that way how could she refuse? "I'm not much of a dancer."

He rose, pulled back her chair and offered his hand. "*Pas un problème.* I will guide you. Relax. I am not going to devour you before dessert."

But after dessert, then what? She wanted to ask, but she was too overwhelmed by his proximity to form the words. He laced his fingers through hers and rested their joined hands over his heart. She could feel the steady thump against her knuckles. He looped his other arm around her waist, spreading his palm over the base of her spine and pressing his chin to her temple. He held her as close as a lover with his thighs brushing hers. *Too close.* She tried to retreat, but the muscles hidden beneath his expensive suit flexed and held fast.

Her breath quickened. His scent, a blend of tangy lime and something totally masculine filled her nostrils. Her mouth dried and her skin steamed. She could barely hear the music to which he swayed over her thudding heart. Regardless of how unwise it might be she could feel herself weakening and wanting to give in to the desire that welled inside her each time he was near.

Pressing her palm against his lapel, she angled her upper body away from his. The move had the unfortunate consequence of aligning their faces. His mouth was much too near. If she rose on her tiptoes she could—

No. She couldn't.

"Where is the music coming from?"

His indulgent half smile sent a spiral of need through her. "There is a string quartet on the terrace."

He danced her through the open doors and then raised his arm for her to spin, but instead of letting her turn a full circle he caught her with her back to his chest and held her facing the flower-filled courtyard below the balcony.

Stacy gasped at the hot length of him spooning her back and then she lifted her gaze from the couples whirling around the flagstone dance floor and the air left her lungs in a long, appreciative, "Wow."

The rocky terrain of Monaco spread out in front of her. One thing about having a country clinging to the side of the mountain was that no matter where you looked you had a postcard-worthy view. Lights twinkled on the landscape like constellations blanketing a clear night sky, and in the distance she could see a brightly lit cruise ship anchored in the harbor. "It's beautiful."

His breath stirred the hair at her temple a second before his lips touched her skin. "And so are you."

He cupped her shoulders and turned her to face him. His palms glided down her arms and then he grasped the railing on either side of her, caging her between a twenty-foot drop and temptation. Either one could leave her broken. The warmth of the iron railing pressed her back, but the heat of his hips and thighs against hers set her afire. He feathered a kiss on one corner of her mouth and then the other. Teasing, fleeting, tantalizing kisses. Insubstantial and unsatisfying.

Her insides quivered and she wanted more. She wanted him to kiss her—to really kiss her—in a way she'd never wanted any man before, and that was dangerous territory. It had to be Madeline's talk of a vacation affair making Stacy yearn for what she couldn't have.

"Come home with me tonight, Stacy. *Je veux faire l'amour avec toi.*"

I want to make love with you. Blood rushed to her head and then drained with dizzying speed to settle low in her belly. She closed her eyes, bit her lip and shook her head. "I can't."

But she wanted to. She really, *really* wanted to. Sex had never been the exciting event for her that everyone claimed it was. She had a feeling it *would* be with Franco, but he was exactly the kind of man she'd sworn to avoid.

"*Non?* Because even though your mouth tells me no, this—" his head bent and his lips scorched a brief kiss over the frantically beating pulse in her neck "—this says yes."

Torn between desire and common sense she pressed her palms against his chest and prayed for the strength to keep refusing. A flash of movement beyond his shoulder caught her eye. She sent up a silent thank-you for the reprieve. "The waiter is back."

Ever so slowly Franco straightened, but the banked fires in his eyes promised "later." He released his hold on the railing beside her, stepped back and gestured for her to precede him into the room. Her legs were almost too weak to carry her.

Close call. Good thing this was their one and only date because she doubted she could continue saying no.

And saying yes would be far too dangerous.

"What is it you want, Stacy?"

Stacy's yearning expression as she gazed at the moonless midnight sky hit Franco with the impact of a sailboat boom. Whatever it was she wanted, he wanted to give it to her. Within reason, of course. And he would reap the rewards for his generosity.

She stopped in the corner of Hôtel Reynard's garden. "What do you mean?"

Why her? Why did this woman arouse him so easily? He didn't have the answer to the question he'd been asking himself since seeing her outside Midas yesterday, but he would find it. Sipping from her soft, fragrant skin at the restaurant tonight had only whetted his appetite. "What is it you wish for when you look upon the stars?"

"What makes you think I'm wishing for anything?"

"Your eyes give you away."

She bit her lip and hesitated. "Financial security."

"Money?" He almost spat the word. It always came down to money, but he had expected Stacy to at least make an attempt to hide her greed. Disappointment dampened his satisfaction over being right about her. Had he believed Stacy was different from any of his father's ex-wives or from his own? *Non.* Life had taught him a hard lesson. All women were the same. Yes, they came in different sizes, shapes and colors, but the craving for money is what made their mercenary hearts beat. And Stacy's greed played directly into his hands.

"My mother struggled to make ends meet when I was a child. Sometimes she had to choose between rent and food. Until I landed the job with the accounting firm I wasn't in much better shape, and now I—" She turned her back abruptly and dipped her fingers into the fountain. "I don't ever want to be in that position again."

"Your father?"

Her spine stiffened and her hands fisted. "Not part of the picture."

The personal insights—of which she'd shared few during dinner—softened him and he couldn't afford sentimentality. Time to close the deal. "And if I could offer you that financial security?"

"What do you mean?" She frowned at him over her shoulder. "Are you offering me a job?"

He joined her beside the fountain. "I am offering

you a million euros to be my mistress for the remainder of your time in Monaco. One month, is it not?"

Shock parted her lips and widened her eyes. "You're joking."

"*Non.* I realize you have obligations to Candace and Vincent, but the remainder of your time would be mine. There will be no declarations of love. No false promises. Just passion and for you, profit. *Tu comprends?*"

She shook her head as if confused. "No, I don't understand. Are you offering to pay me to sleep with you? *Like a prostitute?*"

"In France, being a man's mistress is a respected position."

"I'm not French. And sex for money is still sex for money. I'm not for sale, Monsieur Constantine. Not by the hour. Or the week. Or the month." She hugged her wrap closer and backed away without taking her gaze from his.

He pursued for each step she retreated. Nothing worth having ever came easily. And contrarily, while he respected her for not accepting his first offer, her avarice angered him. She wanted him and she wanted the money. The flutter of her pulse, the rapidity of her breathing and those very expressive eyes gave her away. Why deny it? Why deny them both?

"Why not profit from the chemistry between us, Stacy? You would be doubly rewarded. With the pleasure I can give you and with the financial security you crave."

She reached the end of the path both figuratively and literally. A low stone wall blocked her escape. Franco had restrained himself all evening, but he no longer could. He lifted a hand and stroked his knuckles along her cheekbone. "I promise you pleasure, Stacy."

She inhaled a ragged breath, but she didn't jerk away.

He slid his fingers into her silky hair and held her captive as he lowered his head to sample the mouth he'd craved for hours. Her lips were as sweet and soft as he'd imagined—more so. But she stood stiffly in his embrace with her mouth closed and her arms crossed in front of her, clutching the wrap.

Franco wasn't willing to accept defeat. He dragged his fingertips over the clasp of her dress at her nape and down the ridge of her spine. She shivered and her lips parted on a gasp. He swept inside. She tasted delicious, and he couldn't help delving deeper. Pulling her closer, he eased his hand beneath her wrap and caressed the satiny skin of her back.

The tension drained from her rigid muscles on a sigh and she curved into him, nudging her soft breasts into his chest and touching her tongue to his. Her palms flattened against his ribs and then slid to his waist. Victory surged through him, mixing with the desire already pumping through his veins. He stroked downward, curving his hand over her rounded bottom and pulling her flush against his erection.

She stiffened and jerked out of his arms. Her delicious breasts rose and fell rapidly, the tight nipples like tiny pebbles beneath her bodice. "No. I— You— No. I can't. I won't."

But he could see the indecision in her eyes. Whether she wanted to admit it or not, his proposition tempted her. "I will give you twenty-four hours to reconsider. *Au revoir.* Sleep well, *mon gardénia.*"

He would not.

Three

A knock on the bedroom door jarred Stacy from her dream of a deep, velvety voice whispering illicit suggestions to her in French. Groggily, she sat up, finger-combed the hair from her eyes and tried to banish Franco Constantine from her mind. "*Oui?* I mean, come in."

The door opened and Candace breezed in. "*Bonjour.* You're a sleepyhead this morning."

Stacy glanced at the clock. Ten. She'd overslept, but thanks to the thoughts tumbling through her head after Franco's insulting offer, she hadn't fallen asleep until after four. She couldn't believe she'd actually lain awake debating the pros and cons of accepting and mentally converting euros to dollars. Worse, each time she'd dozed off she'd relived his reason-robbing kiss. "Sorry."

"No problem. But I need you to rise and shine. Vincent called. He heard about a villa that's about to come on the market, and he wants me to check it out. I need a second opinion and I know I can count on you to be practical." She perched on the edge of Stacy's bed. "Property sells fast here because there's such a high demand and a limited selection. Vincent's stuck at the new hotel site in Aruba until they work out this labor problem, and he's afraid we'll miss out on a good thing if we don't act fast."

Stacy shoved back the covers. "Then the move to Monaco is definite?"

Candace sighed. "It appears so. Vincent lives here for part of the year when he's not traveling for the hotel, but he says his condo overlooking the port in Fontvieille isn't big enough for three."

Surprise superseded the sinking feeling over the confirmation that Stacy's only friend was moving away. "Three?"

Candace winced. "Oops. I didn't mean to let that slip."

"You're pregnant?"

"Yes. Almost eight weeks. So it's a good thing we're getting married soon, isn't it?"

"I guess so." Stacy rose, but hesitated. "Should I offer my congratulations?"

"Absolutely," Candace said with a grin. She snatched Stacy into a bouncing hug and then released her. "I'm so excited I'm about to burst, but could you not tell anyone? We're not ready for Vincent's family to find out yet. I really shouldn't have said anything. I've been lucky so far because my morning sickness isn't so bad that I can't hide it or claim it's pre-wedding stress, and I can blame the need for naps on our late nights."

"You can trust me to keep your secret."

Trust. There it was again. That word. The one Stacy struggled with. "Give me thirty minutes to shower and dress."

She headed for the bathroom, shed her gown and stepped into the glass shower stall and then dunked her face under the hot spray to wash the grogginess away. The shower pelted her overly sensitized skin, dredging up remnants of dreams best forgotten.

Maybe a short-term affair was the best she could hope for given her trust issues. Should she reconsider Franco's offer? It wasn't as if he'd follow her across the Atlantic to try to force her to come back to him when he wasn't in love with her. And he'd stated up front that all he wanted was a month of her time.

But sex for money is still sex for money.

She lathered, rinsed and then shoved open the etched-glass shower door to glare at the wet woman in the steamy mirror. "I can't believe you are still debating this."

Would you have slept with him if he hadn't sprung this on you? Maybe. Probably. Because when he'd kissed her, saying no had been the last thing on her mind.

She snagged a towel and scrubbed briskly. "Let it go. You're grossly underqualified to be anyone's mistress."

But a million well-invested euros could set you up for life. No more worries about poverty. No more living paycheck to paycheck. And you won't have to panic if you can't find another job right away.

"No. Too risky. I don't have to see him again until the wedding. Forget his obscene offer. Forget him." With that settled she nodded at her reflection and reached for her makeup bag.

Twenty minutes later she zipped on another one of the sundresses she'd bought before getting laid off, this one a knee-length mint green number, stepped into her walking sandals and then yanked open the door to the sitting room and spotted the one man she'd hoped to avoid. Her stomach plunged. "What are you doing here?"

Franco set down his coffee cup and rose from the sofa. His gaze raked her from head to toe in a long, slow sweep, and Stacy couldn't stop hers from doing the same to him. She hadn't seen him in casual clothing before. His white short-sleeved shirt exposed the thick biceps his suits had only hinted at and his belted khakis revealed a flat stomach and narrow hips. A swimmer's body.

"*Bonjour,* Stacy. I am your chauffeur today."

She caught herself watching his lips move as he spoke and remembering how they'd felt against hers, and then his words sank in. Alarm clamored through her. She looked from Franco to Candace sitting in a chair. "What?"

Her friend smiled smugly. "Didn't I mention that Franco is the one who told Vincent about his neighbor's decision to sell?"

"No. You didn't. So you have your second opinion. You don't need me."

"Are you kidding? No offense, Franco, but you're a man. I need a woman's opinion."

He shrugged his wide polo-covered shoulders. "None taken."

Stacy wanted to lock herself in her room. Part of being able to resist his indecent proposition depended on not having temptation shoved in her face at every turn.

"Please, Stacy," Candace wheedled.

Stacy stifled a grimace. How could she refuse when Candace and Vincent were treating her to a month in paradise? Even if she had a sneaking suspicion the request for those consecutive weeks off might have contributed to her getting laid off. "All right."

Franco's broad palm gestured to the tray of pastries on the table. "We will wait for you to eat."

If she put food in her agitated—compliments of Franco—stomach she'd be sick. Stacy poured a glass of orange juice, guzzled it with inelegant haste and then returned her glass to the tray. "I'm ready."

Franco's knowing look made her twitchy. Stacy kept her gaze averted from him as he escorted them downstairs and outside. She could feel his steady regard as they waited for the valet to bring his car around, and when Candace became distracted by something in the hotel gift shop's window and wandered a few yards away he took advantage by moving closer. Stacy's senses went on red alert.

"You slept well?" he asked quietly.

"Of course," she lied without lifting her gaze above the whorl of dark hair exposed by the open neck of his shirt.

"I did not. Desire for you kept me awake. Each breeze through my open window felt like your lips upon my skin."

Her breath caught and her pulse stuttered. She glared at him. "You said I wouldn't have to see you again if I had dinner with you."

"*Non.* I said you wouldn't have to see me alone, *mon gardénia.*"

"Stop that. I am not your anything."

"But you will be." The certainty in his voice rattled her already fragile composure. "I cannot wait to have you in my bed, Stacy."

Were Frenchmen born knowing how to talk a woman out of her clothes? "Don't hold your breath."

An expensive-looking black sedan—Maserati made sedans?—rolled to a stop in front of them. The valet hopped out and circled the car to open the doors for the women while Franco moved to the driver's side. Stacy stepped toward the back, but Candace cut in front of her. "You sit up front. The hairpin turns make me nervous, and my stomach would appreciate the back seat. It's a little dicey this morning," she whispered the last phrase.

No fair playing the morning-sickness card. "Fine."

Stacy slid into the leather passenger seat beside Franco. Even with the console between them in the spacious interior, his presence overpowered her. His hand seemed larger on the gearshift just inches from her knee and his shoulders immense in the enclosed space. She inhaled his cologne with every breath.

He turned his head and their eyes met for heart-stopping seconds. "Fasten your seat belt, Stacy."

She complied with unsteady hands, and then Franco drove away from the coast and wound his way up the rocky mountainside. Although the steep drop-offs had Stacy clutching the sides of her seat, she had to admit the view was breathtaking.

"Do you see Larvotto?" he asked a few moments later. The blue-green Mediterranean glimmered beyond the three crescents of beach.

"Yes," Stacy answered when Candace didn't, and then she twisted in her seat to see her friend's pale face. "Franco, could you open the windows a bit?"

"Bien sûr." He quickly checked the rearview mirror and then the windows silently lowered. Slowing the vehicle, he turned down a tree-lined street which appeared to have been chiseled from the mountainside. "Candace, *tu va bien?*"

"Ah…*oui.* I'm fine." She clearly wasn't. "Are we close?"

He stopped the car in the quiet roadway. "We are here, but my house is two doors over if you need to lie down."

"No. I'll be better once I get out of the car. I keep remembering Princess Grace drove off one of these roads and died."

"Not this one." He turned into a driveway leading to a cream-colored stucco house with a red tiled roof that looked like something from a Mediterranean vacation guide. Stacy climbed from the car and immediately turned to check on Candace.

"Who would have believed pregnancy would give me vertigo?" Candace whispered. She linked arms with Stacy and followed Franco down the stone path to the front entrance. He pulled a key from his pocket and unlocked the door.

Stacy balked. "There's no real estate agent?"

"*Non.* My neighbor has only recently decided to sell. He is abroad, but left me a key."

He gestured for them to precede him. Stacy let Candace go first. Franco caught Stacy's hand and held her back. Her heart stuttered. Was he going to badger her about his offer? Or kiss her again?

"Is this part of the pregnancy?" he asked.

She blinked. "You know?"

"*Oui.* Vincent asked me to keep an eye on her, so you will be seeing a lot of me, Stacy."

Not good news when her plan to resist him was already on shaky ground. She tugged her hand free before the heat of his palm against hers melted her resistance. "She claims the pregnancy is giving her vertigo."

He looked adorably confused. "*C'est possible?*"

"I have no idea. I know nothing about being pregnant."

He nodded and then escorted her inside. To Stacy, who'd lived in low-budget accommodations all her life, the home looked like something from the *Architectural Digest* magazines her accounting firm—*former* firm— kept in the waiting area. Talk about lifestyles of the rich and famous…. She couldn't even begin to guess how many millions of euros this place cost.

She trailed after Candace who'd apparently recovered enough to examine one gorgeous room after another in the spacious home. When the women returned to the living room where Franco waited, he pushed open the door to the terrace behind the house. Candace wandered off to explore every nook and cranny of the gardens.

Stacy stayed on the flagstone patio, letting her eyes devour the flower-filled landscape. She had only vague memories of the landscaped yard of the house she'd lived in until she was eight. The places she and her mother had lived afterward had been barren and devoid of color. One day, Stacy vowed, she'd own a home a fraction as beautiful as this. One terrace of the two-level lot held a large pool, and another, a maze of roses. Living here would be a fantasy come true. And the view—

"C'est incroyable, non?" Franco said directly behind her seconds before his muscular frame spooned her back. His arms surrounded her and his fingers laced through hers on the iron railing, holding her captive when she would have ducked away.

He had to stop doing that. Every feminine particle in her urged her to lean into him and relish in the novel sensations he sent bubbling through her, but her survival instincts screamed *Run, danger ahead.* The emotional push-pull left her breathless and disoriented.

"But my view is better. You will see," he added in a deep voice that stroked her skin like a caress, peaked her nipples and made her quiver. "Come, we must go. Candace looks in need of a chaise and a cool drink."

He stepped away, taking his body heat with him and leaving Stacy surprisingly chilled in the warm late-morning air. How could she be so affected by a man she barely knew?

Candace had indeed paled as she slowly climbed the

stairs to the main patio. Stacy crossed to her side, but her friend waved away her concern as they returned to the car.

Stacy struggled to fortify her resistance to Franco as they pulled onto the road, but her internal alarms shrieked when he slowed the vehicle and turned into a driveway two doors down. "Is this your house? Why are we coming here?"

"Did I forget to tell you Franco invited us for coffee?" Candace asked from the back seat.

Stacy turned to scowl at her. "Yes. You did."

"Oops." There was no *oops* about it. The bride was matchmaking and not at all subtly.

"How kind of him." Not kind. Manipulative.

The satisfied smile playing about Franco's delectable lips made Stacy seethe. He'd wanted her in his home and he'd manipulated circumstances to make it happen. The man was set on seduction, and she had a sinking feeling he wasn't thwarted often or easily. And then she spotted his house and gasped.

The large two-story rectangular villa had been painted a buttery yellow. The trim on the second-floor balcony and around the arched windows gleamed white in the morning light. "Palladian style, right? How old?"

"Correct. The original structure was built in 1868. It has been renovated many times. Most recently by me. You have studied architecture, Stacy?"

"No. I just like to read."

Candace scooted forward. "Stacy's a bit of a history buff. She devoured any research material on Monaco and the Mediterranean she could get her hands on before our trip."

A blush warmed Stacy's cheeks. "Your home's beautiful, Franco."

"*Merci*. Wait until you see the inside. And the gardens,

of course. They are lovely by moonlight." His gaze held hers and last night's invitation lingered in his eyes. She would have seen his gardens by moonlight if she'd come home with him after dinner. She still could if she became his mistress.

Her heart accelerated and her mouth dried. "Too bad we'll miss that."

The twitch of his lips as he climbed from the car said he hadn't missed her sarcasm, and then Candace poked Stacy's shoulder. "Cut it out."

Stacy twisted in her seat. "Quit matchmaking."

The car doors opened. Franco stood in the driveway. "Mesdemoiselles?"

He helped them from the car and then turned toward the house. Stacy caught herself admiring the fit of his trousers over the tight globes of his derriere as she followed him up the stone walk toward the covered front entrance. European men wore pants that fit—none of that super-baggy stuff American guys currently favored. The fitted style certainly suited Franco.

After unlocking the tall arched door he motioned for them to enter with the sweep of his arm. Candáce led the way. Stacy reluctantly followed with Franco on her heels. She couldn't help feeling that by entering his domain she was crossing a point of no return.

Her first impression was one of high ceilings and sun-drenched spaces rolling on and on in acres of cool, glossy white marble floors. Wide arches divided the individual rooms, but the glass-paned doors to each stood open. To her left a suspended staircase circled upward, and in front of her a pair of round marble columns separated a foyer bigger than her den back home from a living room larger than her entire apartment.

She glanced at Franco and found him watching her intently. "Welcome to my home."

"It's um…" Gorgeous. Huge. Intimidating. "Very nice."

The million euros he'd offered her should have been a clue to Franco's wealth, but she'd had no idea he was filthy rich. Most women would find his affluence a turn-on. But for Stacy it had the opposite effect.

"We will have refreshments on the terrace." He led them through the living room. Stacy trailed Candace past the dark wooden tables that interspersed the black leather sofas and chairs. Woven carpets in shades of ivory, black and red dotted the floor.

Red. Like blood on the white floor. She shuddered and skirted around the rugs.

Curved floor-to-ceiling French doors punctuated the exterior wall revealing an expansive patio that put the last home's to shame. Franco opened one of the doors. His bare forearm brushed Stacy's as she passed through. Accidental? Doubtful. Awareness trickled over her. She moved into the sunshine to bake the goose bumps away.

Candace crossed directly to the swimming pool located at the far end of the stone terrace and leaned over the railing. "Stacy, you have to see this. The pool pours over the side of the patio in a waterfall."

"It empties into a whirlpool below," Franco told her and then he moved closer to Stacy, dipped his head until his breath teased her ear. "Half of the spa is concealed beneath the house by the falling water. I would like to make love to you there."

Stunned by his sneak attack, Stacy struggled to catch her breath and formulate a prickly reply, but her brain refused to cooperate. Her heart raced and her palms moistened. Her skin flushed hot and then cold when she realized that in the split second before reason intervened she'd wanted to make love with him too.

That kiss clearly addled your thinking.

"Make Candace sit and rest," he murmured quietly along with a brief, but electrifying caress over the curve of her waist. "I will return with refreshments momentarily." He went inside.

Shakily, Stacy crossed to the railing. Not because she wanted to see the whirlpool below and visualize the decadent scene Franco had planted in her head. No, definitely not that. She looked because the view of Monte Carlo and Larvotto Beach from Franco's patio was more beautiful than any of the postcards she'd bought as souvenirs of her trip.

To her right a stone staircase wound down to the lower level of the terraced yard. Trees and flowers dappled the lush slope of green grass with shadows and brilliant splashes of color. And fight as she might, Stacy couldn't prevent her gaze from dropping to the exposed half of the spa.

Why not? You want to.

She'd have to be crazy to risk it. From what she'd seen of his home Franco had to be ten times wealthier than she'd suspected. *And ten times sexier. He arouses you with nothing more than words. Why not give those big hands a try? It's not like you're ever going to let yourself fall in love with anyone. So why hold out?*

"Amazing, isn't it?" Candace interrupted Stacy's illicit thoughts. "I can't imagine living like this."

Stacy pushed aside the tantalizing images. "Neither can I. It must be a real power rush to have enough money to buy whatever you want. We should find a shady spot to sit and wait for Franco."

"He knows about the baby, doesn't he? Did you tell him?" Candace asked as they strolled toward the shady covered loggia.

"Yes, he knows. Vincent told him."

"I should have guessed Vincent would. He's very protective, and he would trust Franco not to betray our little secret." Candace plopped onto a rattan lounge chair covered by a deep white cushion, lay back and closed her eyes. "Wouldn't it be great to live in paradise like this only two doors apart?"

Stacy chose a chair. She couldn't relax in Franco's home—not with him stalking her like a predatory beast. And then Candace's meaning sank in. "There's nothing like that between Franco and me."

"Oh please. He undresses you with his eyes whenever he thinks I'm not looking. You can't tell me you haven't noticed."

Stacy *had* noticed, and she was ashamed to admit the desire simmering in Franco's gaze sent a reciprocal surge through her. At least she assumed that achy, itchy tension was desire. No one had ever made her feel as attractive or feminine in her life, and she'd certainly never looked at a man and wondered how his hands would feel on her body. What would it be like to experience that kind of passion? Did she dare risk it?

"Sex is all he wants."

"Honey, that's all any man wants at first." Candace yawned.

"True. But I'm not looking for a husband."

"Then why not do as Madeline suggested and enjoy what Franco's offering? Other than Vincent, Franco is unquestionably the sexiest man I've ever met. My God, his accent just melts me, and you have to admit he's not hard on the eyes. You'll never get a chance to live like this again. I confess I'm thoroughly enjoying the five-star treatment. But I wish Vincent was here."

Stacy wanted to tell Candace about Franco's insulting proposition, but she didn't dare because telling her friend meant confessing how tempting Stacy found the offer. "Doesn't Vincent's wealth ever…concern you?"

Candace rolled to her side and met Stacy's gaze. "You mean do I worry that he'll use his money and influence to hurt me? No, I don't. I trust Vincent. Stacy, you haven't said much about your past, but from the bits you've let slip I'm guessing some rich guy did a number on you. Whoever he was, you can't let him screw up the rest of your life. Not all rich men are jerks. And you know, I don't think you've dated or gotten laid since I met you. Aren't you overdue?"

"I've dated." Twice, in three years. Pitiful. But sex? No. She needed more than a couple of dates to let her guard down with someone. If she ever could. And now that she thought about it, she probably never had, which was very likely the reason her last brief relationship had ended.

"Stacy, you've heard my sob story about the visiting surgeon who wooed me, bedded me and then returned home to the wife and kids I didn't know he had. Loving and losing that jerk burned me, but then I met Vincent and realized that sometimes you have to trust your heart and move on or be stuck in the past forever." Candace yawned again. "Do you mind if I close my eyes until Franco gets back?"

"No, go ahead." Questions and doubts tumbled through Stacy's mind. Was she stuck in the past? Had she given her father and that one tragic night too much power over her life? Or was she merely being prudent? If she didn't face her fears would she continue running from them indefinitely? Running, the way she and her mother had done for eleven years of Stacy's life. After losing her mother, Stacy had sworn she'd stop running and put down roots.

Roots a million euros could buy.

She stared at the pool and the water pouring over the ledge. She'd said no to Franco's proposition and she'd meant it. Deep in her heart she knew sleeping with him for the money was the wrong thing to do, but her practical side couldn't completely dismiss the idea of a lifetime of financial security in return for a month of intimacy with a man she desired like no other.

The mental debate circled her thoughts like an annoying, persistent mosquito no matter how often she swatted it away. Was Franco's offer too good to be true or was this an opportunity to put her past to bed and secure her future?

Trusting him when she barely knew him went against everything her mother had taught her about being wary of strangers. If only she had more time to discover whether power and money had corrupted Franco, but he'd given her only twenty-four hours to make a life-altering decision. Half of those hours had already passed.

The rattle of crockery drew her gaze to Franco crossing the terrace with a tray in his hands. His biceps bulged under the weight. He paused, his gaze landing on Candace. "She sleeps?"

Candace didn't stir. Stacy shrugged. "I guess so."

He nodded toward the house, turned and retraced his path. Stacy hesitated, but then rose and followed. Franco's kitchen was a combination of old-world charm and modern convenience—a cook's dream of dark cabinetry, glossy countertops and top-of-the-line appliances.

The aroma of freshly brewed coffee filled the air. He set the tray on the table. "You did not eat breakfast. You must be hungry."

She studied the array of fruits, cheeses and chocolates. He also had a coffee carafe, a pitcher of orange juice and a couple of bottles of sparkling water. "Your housekeeper did this?"

"You think I am not capable of feeding my guests?"

"I don't know you well enough to know what to think." And therein lay the crux of her dilemma. Part of her wanted to explore the way he made her feel and part of her wanted to play it safe.

"My housekeeper comes twice a week. The rest of the time I fend for myself. Eat, please. Or would you prefer I feed you?" He lifted a candy. "These are the chocolate-covered cherries you enjoyed the day we met. I would like to taste it on your tongue."

Her breath snagged. She staggered back a step, but that wasn't nearly far enough. She needed a break from his overwhelming charisma because she was perilously close to caving. "I need the restroom."

"*Bien sûr.* This way." He popped the chocolate into his mouth and led her down a hall, through a set of arched double doors, and he then stepped aside and gestured to another door. *"C'est là."*

Stacy stood frozen in what could only be Franco's bedroom. A huge wooden bed covered in a red-and-gold nubby silk spread dominated the otherwise black-and-white space. "You, uh…don't have a guest bathroom?"

"Of course, but I wanted to see you in my bedroom, and I wanted you, *mon gardénia,* to imagine yourself in my bed and in my bath with my hands and my mouth on your skin. As I have done."

The tantalizing vision exploded in her mind in vivid

Technicolor, and a fine tremor rippled over her. Her heart hammered and her mouth dried.

Franco didn't attempt to touch her or coerce her by using the desire clearly visible in his blue eyes. He'd simply stated his wishes and left the rest to her.

One step and she'd have financial security for life and a lover who might possibly make sex enjoyable rather than endurable. And when she left there'd be an ocean between them.

She closed her eyes and inhaled deeply.

Play it safe? Or risk it all?

Four

"Okay. You win, Franco. I'll be your mistress for a month. But I have conditions," Stacy added before Franco could speak. She dodged when he reached for her. There was no way she could think with his hands on her.

Cynicism replaced the triumphant spark in his eyes. He leaned against the doorjamb and folded his arms over his broad chest. Cocky. Arrogant. Male. "And they are?"

She had to be insane to agree to this, but if she hoped to survive it then she had to maintain some control and keep the affair on a business footing. What she needed were boundaries and rules. Safeguards. With her heart racing, she dampened her lips.

"I don't want Candace, Amelia and Madeline to know about the money." Or any chance of friendship would be destroyed. She wasn't even sure she could respect herself once this was over. She hadn't had to go hungry or bail on a landlord in the middle of the night since her mother's death, but the memories of the hunger pains and furtive escapes of her childhood lingered. And then there was her current employment— *un*employment—status to deal with once she returned home. She'd had excellent reviews at work, but still, the job market was tight and hers wasn't the only company downsizing. Add in a dwindling saving account and...

Focus on the future. With careful investing you'll never be poor or homeless again.

He inclined his head. "Anything else?"

"I won't spend the night." Call her crazy, but she didn't want to let her guard down enough to literally sleep with him.

A single dark eyebrow lifted. *"Non?"*

"No. My duty is first and foremost to Candace. We begin most days going over the wedding planning stuff. My time with you can't interfere with that."

"I shall return you to the hotel before your morning meetings."

Suddenly, she felt dirty. "When and how will I get paid?"

His nostrils flared and his generous lips thinned. "Your bridesmaid duties will end when Vincent and Candace depart on their honeymoon trip following the reception. You are scheduled to leave Monaco the next day, *oui?*"

"Oui. I mean, yes."

"You will spend your last night in Monaco with me. The entire night, Stacy." It was an order not a question. "In the morning I will give you a cashier's check and drive you to the airport, but should you not fulfill any part of our agreement, then no money."

Her breath hitched and her pulse thumped as loudly as the helicopter taxi they'd taken to Monaco from the Nice-Côte d'Azur airport. "And if you decide to end it early?"

A muscle in his jaw bunched and then his lips curled in a slow, devastatingly sexy smile. "I assure you I never finish anything prematurely."

It took a second for his meaning to sink in and when it did her cheeks caught fire. "But if you do?"

"You will be paid."

"Okay." Now what? Did they shake hands over the deal or—

Franco captured her elbows and tugged her forward. His mouth slanted over hers in a hard kiss as if she'd angered him. Stacy stiffened as second, third and fourth thoughts descended like an avalanche. She was on the verge of pulling away and cancelling their arrangement when his lips softened and parted. The fingers grasping her arms loosened and swept up to sift through her hair and cradle her head in his hands.

His mouth lifted, realigned and returned, seducing a response from her with long, luxurious turn-her-muscles-to-mush kisses. She tasted a hint of dark chocolate on his tongue. Chocolate and Franco, a hot and heady combination. His hands painted warm stripes down her back, over her hips and then around to her waist, before rising until his thumbs rested just below her bra.

Her breasts ached in anticipation of his touch, and desire simmered inside her. She couldn't believe her body could respond with such abandon when she knew Franco was using her. She'd been used before. But she wasn't a lonely seventeen-year-old trying to fit in at her third high school anymore. She wouldn't expect love or forever this time, so she wouldn't be hurt.

"Hey guys, where'd you go?" Candace's voice called out from somewhere in the house.

Franco slowly lifted his head, his lips clinging to

Stacy's for several heartbeats. His passion-darkened gaze speared hers. "Tonight we begin."

She couldn't find her voice, but she managed a stiff nod.

Dear God, what had she done?

She'd agreed to trade sex for security. She couldn't help feeling she'd sold her soul to the devil, and she hoped she didn't live to regret it.

Anticipation made Franco edgy. He hated it. He was, after all, a man of thirty-eight and not a boy of eighteen. His hormones did not seem to know the difference tonight.

Impatience urged him to take Stacy directly to his bedroom, to strip away her modest black dress and cover her ivory skin with his hands and mouth, but her pale, anxious expression cooled his ardor. Standing in his foyer, she looked torn between running back into the night and fulfilling her end of the bargain no matter how unpleasant.

Where was the passionate but reserved woman he'd left at the hotel mere hours ago? The one who'd kissed him with such fervor this morning that only her friend's untimely interruption had prevented him from consummating their agreement against his bedroom door? He wanted that passionate woman back. And he would have her. Stacy would be warm and pliant in his arms and his bed before the night ended. And he would win. The woman. And the contest with his father.

He pitched his keys onto the credenza, halted behind her and curved his hands over her shoulders. She startled. "May I take your wrap?"

"Oh, um, yes, sure." She darted a quick, nervous glance at him and tension tightened inside him as an unacceptable thought pierced his conscience.

"Stacy, are you a virgin?" He'd had lovers, dozens of them, but no virgins. Experienced women understood that all he wanted was the transitory pleasure of their bodies. An innocent might expect more.

Color rushed to her cheeks and she ducked her chin. "No. But I...this...is new to me. I don't know where to begin."

His clenched muscles loosened. Nerves he could handle. Regrets and crying, he could not. He had intended to satisfy his hunger for Stacy first tonight and then his less demanding appetite for dinner afterward, but perhaps he would alter his strategy. Dinner first. Pleasure later. Anticipation would only heighten the senses. "Leave that to me."

Franco stroked the lace down her arms, caught her elbows and pulled her back against his front. Her bottom nudged his thighs. The urge to thrust his growing arousal against her gnawed at him, but he would coax Stacy until she was breathless and eager for his possession, as she had been earlier. He nuzzled through her silky hair and sipped from the warm, fragrant juncture of her neck and shoulder. She shivered.

Bien, the responsive woman still lurked beneath her pale and tense exterior. He encircled her with his arms and spread his palms over the slight curve of her abdomen. "I will ensure your pleasure tonight, *mon gardénia.*"

A little *hic* of breath lifted her breasts, and though he wanted to cup her soft flesh in his hands and stroke his thumbs over the tips pushing against the fabric of her dress, he could wait. But not long.

"We will dine on the terrace." He released her and led her through the living room, draping her wrap over the back of a chair as they passed. On the patio he seated her, lit the candles he'd placed in the center of the table and then poured the cabernet franc. After removing the lid covering the crudités and setting it aside, he sat and lifted his glass. *"À nous et aux plaisirs de la nuit."*

She made a choked sound. "I'm sorry?"

"To us and the pleasures of the night," he translated.

"That's what I thought you said," she muttered into the bowl of her glass and took a healthy sip of wine.

He removed a small box from his suit pocket and placed it on the table in front of her. He had planned to give her this after savoring her delicious body, but why wait? Stacy needed coaxing, and in his experience jewelry always made women more amenable. "For you."

The line formed between her eyebrows. "You don't have to buy presents for me."

He would make sure she wore it when she met his father. He shrugged. "Open it."

She set aside her wine, hesitantly opened the box and stared. Seconds later she snapped the lid closed and shoved the box toward him. "I can't accept that."

He stilled. "You don't like diamonds?"

"Of course, but—"

"You have a diamond bracelet?"

"No." She closed her eyes, swallowed and then met his gaze. "Franco, we already have a deal. Can we just stick to it?"

He masked his surprise and puzzlement. He had never had a woman refuse his gifts before—especially not expensive jewelry. "Perhaps I wish to see you wearing the diamonds. And nothing else."

"Oh." Her cheeks flushed. "*Oh,*" she repeated and fiddled with the stem of her glass for a moment before looking at him through her thick lashes. It was a worried glance rather than a flirtatious one. "Diamonds do it for you, huh?"

He reared back. "No, diamonds do not *do it for me*. I merely wished to give you a gift."

"And I'm telling you that you don't have to."

What game was she playing? He examined her face, her guileless eyes. Was her innocence an act? It had to be. Otherwise she never would have accepted his offer. He rose. "I will return momentarily with dinner."

In the kitchen he mechanically plated the smoked mozzarella with sundried tomatoes and peppercorns in a puddle of olive oil while mulling over Stacy's refusal. She had to have an ulterior motive. He retrieved the filet *barole* from the warming oven, divided it onto dishes and poured the cognac and mushroom sauce over it.

Was she after a bigger prize? Perhaps a diamond ring instead of a bracelet? If so, she would not get one from him. He would never marry again. His one and only failed marriage had taught him that women were selfish creatures. Nothing mattered except their wants. *Nothing*.

Not even life.

His throat tightened at the memory of the babe his wife had carelessly discarded without his knowledge or consent. Had there not been complications with the abortion, causing the doctors to hospitalize Lisette and call Franco to Paris, he would never have known her "shopping trip" was a lie or that she had conceived his child—a child she did not want. And then there were his father's costly divorces. Stacy was no different from any other greedy woman. She had revealed her true nature by accepting his terms. He set his jaw.

Non. He did not trust women. He enjoyed them *briefly* and then he moved on. But he was a generous lover both in bed and out. Stacy would have no complaints.

Stacy was not at the table when he carried the tray outside. He scanned the dimly lit terrace and found her in the shadows by the railing overlooking the garden below. Or perhaps she studied the whirlpool. His arousal stirred in anticipation.

After placing the meal on the table he joined her. "Dinner waits."

She turned slightly. A gentle breeze lifted tendrils of hair. "I'm sorry, Franco. I didn't mean to hurt your feelings by refusing the bracelet. I just don't think we should try to make this into something it's not."

Again she surprised and perplexed him. "What would that be?"

"A relationship."

His thoughts exactly, but hearing her voice them disturbed him in an inexplicable way. "We are going to be lovers, Stacy. We will have a relationship, albeit a temporary one. And if I choose to buy things for you then I do so because it pleases me, not because I expect more from you than our original agreement. Now come. We will eat and then we will pursue our mutual pleasure."

Would she be worth a million bucks?

Stacy's stomach clenched. She had absolutely no appetite and her taste buds had deserted her, but she forced down another bite of tender steak to drag out the meal as long as possible. Throughout dinner she'd watched Franco's hands as he cut his meat or cradled his wineglass, and her mind had raced ahead. Those hands would soon be on her. Cupping her flesh. Stroking her skin. Was that anticipation or dread making her dizzy?

What if after they did this Franco decided she wasn't worth the money? After all, she wasn't experienced. She could count her intimate encounters on one hand, and her knowledge was limited to the basics—which in her opinion were overrated. If he expected anything like the fancy stuff she'd read about in the women's magazines she'd borrowed from work, then he'd be disappointed.

Franco placed his knife and fork on his empty plate. "The food is not to your liking?"

Chew. Chew. Chew. Gulp. "It's delicious. Did you cook?"

His knowing eyes called her a liar. "No. It is catered. Perhaps your appetite lies elsewhere."

Her fork slipped, the tines screeching across the china. She winced. Franco had probably never encountered a more gauche female. He was sexy and sophisticated down to the soles of his shoes and she was…not. So why had he chosen her?

She abandoned her utensils, blotted her mouth with her cloth napkin and then knotted her fingers in her lap. "I guess I'm just not very hungry."

"I am ravenous." He abruptly pushed back his chair and stood. "But not for food."

Stacy's heart stalled and then raced, but Franco reached for their plates instead of her, piled them on the tray and carried them toward the kitchen.

Time's up. Time to deliver your end of the bargain.

Stacy slowly exhaled and then lurched into action, nearly overturning her glass in the process. She gathered the stemware and then followed Franco inside, wishing she'd drunk more than one glass of wine. If she had, maybe she wouldn't be so nervous. But she'd never acquired a taste for wine. She preferred girly drinks with umbrellas, and she drank precious few of those because she kept herself on a strict budget. Unfortunately, sobriety left her tense and clear-headed enough to doubt her sanity in accepting his proposition. Besides, getting drunk would be stupid. She needed to stay in control.

Whatever had possessed her to believe she was qualified to be Franco's mistress? How could she satisfy a worldly man like him? And how could she become intimate with a man she barely knew? Franco wasn't much of a talker. If he'd shared half as much conversation as he had lingering, desire-laden, toe-curling glances, then she could write an in-depth biography about him. But he hadn't. Then again, neither had she.

Details aren't necessary. This isn't about friendship or forever.

Stacy stiffened her spine. She could get through this. She'd survived attending fourteen schools in ten years, her mother's shocking and unexpected death and her father's betrayal. Four weeks as Franco's plaything would grant her the economic freedom to buy a home and to stop feeling like a visitor in her own life—a visitor who might have to pack up and leave at any moment.

But thinking about the money made her feel a little like a hooker. A lot like one, actually. So she shoved those thoughts aside and tried to focus on the man. About how sexy and desirable Franco made her feel…

When she wasn't thinking about the money. She winced.

Franco deposited the tray beside the sink and then took the goblets from her and set them on the counter.

"Let me help you wash those," she offered, hoping to buy time.

"The dishes can wait. I cannot."

Before Stacy could do more than blink, Franco's arms surrounded her and his mouth crashed onto hers. Possessive. Hungry. Demanding. He cupped her bottom, pulling her flush against the length of his hot muscle-packed body, and his tongue found hers, stroking, tasting, tangling. Arousal simmered beneath

Stacy's skin, but it couldn't completely overcome her stomach-tightening trepidation or doubts.

Franco was a wealthy, powerful man who had the money to buy whatever he wanted—including her. Would he play by the rules? She was on foreign territory here—both in Monaco and in this affair. Who would protect her if this turned ugly?

She pushed against his chest, breaking the kiss. "Wait."

"For?" His barely audible growl swept across her damp lips, and his passion-darkened eyes bored into hers.

She licked her lips and tasted him. "What if I don't meet your expectations?"

"I find that unlikely." His hand covered her breast, his thumbnail unerringly finding and caressing her nipple with a back and forth motion.

Tendrils of sensation snaked through her defenses. She had to stay clear and focused. Letting go meant becoming vulnerable. Perhaps she should just take care of him? But how? Drop to her knees and take him in her mouth? If so, she had a problem, because her one and only experience with that in high school had not gone well. She shuddered.

He gripped her upper arms and set her from him. "Stacy, what game are you playing?"

"I'm not playing a game. I just…" She bit her bottom lip. "We don't know each other very well."

"What is there to know except the pleasure we can give one another?" His fingers threaded through her hair, tugging gently and tipping her head back. "Have you never experienced immediate attraction for someone you have just met and let passion lead?"

"Uh…no."

His eyes narrowed suspiciously. "How old are you?"

"Twenty-nine. But I, um…"

"You haven't had many lovers."

Was it obvious? Heat scalded her cheeks. She wanted to hide her face, but his grip on her hair prevented it. "No."

His nostrils flared. "I will teach you what pleases me, and I will satisfy you, *mon gardénia*."

He stated it with surety and she wanted to believe him, but why would he bother? He'd bought her whether she liked sex with him or not. "If you say so. You probably should have asked about my sexual experience before offering your bargain."

"*Ce n'est pas important.*"

Not important? How could her lack of experience be unimportant?

He released her hair and laced his fingers through hers. "Come. The kitchen is not the best place for our first time."

Nerves twisted tighter in her stomach with each step. She knew where they were headed long before they reached the carved double wooden doors. His bedroom. Once inside the large chamber he faced her. "I have pictured you here. Sprawled on my sheets. Naked except for the flush of passion on your skin."

She wheezed in a breath at the sensual image his words painted and blurted, "Do you have condoms? Because I'm not on the pill."

"And even if you were, the pill is not protection against sexually transmitted diseases—of which I have none," he stated matter-of-factly.

Her discomfort with the current conversation further illustrated her lack of qualifications to become Franco's mistress. A more experienced woman could probably have this preliminary chat without as much as a blush. But not her. She shifted on her feet. "Me neither."

"I have protection." He turned her toward the bed,

reached for the zip of her dress, swiftly pulled it down to her hips and then flicked her bra open.

Oh God, were they going to just do it? She shouldn't be surprised or disappointed. Despite what the magazines said, in her experience, that's the way it happened. Rushed, fumbling hands followed by awkward contact and grunting. At least it would be over soon.

Air cooled her skin and then warm hands slipped inside the gaping fabric of her dress to trail down her spine with a feather-light touch. Goose bumps rose on her skin and her toes curled in her pumps.

Franco's thumbs worked upward from her lower back, massaging her knotted muscles all the way to her neck. His fingers drew ever-widening circles over her shoulders, down to her waist and back again. Her eyelids grew heavy and she shivered as unexpected pleasure rippled over her.

A hot, open-mouthed kiss on her nape surprised a gasp from her, and then her dress and bra fell from her shoulders. Startled by the swift disrobing, she grabbed at her clothing, but too late. The garments puddled around her ankles. She crossed her arms over her chest, covering her breasts.

"*Non.* Do not hide."

Her eyelids jerked open. She found her gaze locked with Franco's in the large gold-leaf mirror hanging over the dresser. Slowly, painfully, she lowered her hands and fisted her fingers beside her. Her heart pumped harder as his gaze devoured her breasts, her black hipster panties and then her legs. In her opinion, her body was okay, her breasts merely average, but if Franco was disappointed in what he'd bought he didn't show it.

Behind her, he discarded his coat and tie, tossing both toward a chair without breaking her gaze. His belt whistled free and then thumped into the chair. Each movement stirred the air around them and teased the fine hairs on her body. He unbuttoned his cuffs and then his shirt and tugged his shirttails free, but didn't remove the garment. Part of her wanted to turn and examine him as he had her, but the governing part of her stood trans-fixed, muscles locked and rigid.

"*Tu es très* sexy, Stacy." His hands, shades darker than her pale skin, curved around her waist.

Her lungs failed, but whooshed back into action when his palms splayed over her belly, one above her navel and one below. An unaccustomed urge to shift until his hot hands covered more intimate territory per-colated through her, but she remained as still as a statue.

"Your skin is like ivory. You do not sunbathe?" he whispered against the sensitive skin beneath her ear a second before his lips made electrifying contact.

"I d-don't have the time. When I'm not working I volunteer my time mentoring at-risk teens." Kids who were lonely outsiders like she'd been.

His gaze searched hers for a moment and then lowered to the tiny birthmark above her right hip bone. He traced the small reddish splotch with a fingertip. The delicate caress made her feminine muscles clench.

His mouth opened over her skin, laving her pulse point. At the same time he pulled her back against his bare chest. She hardly had time to register the heat of him seeping into her or the tickle of his chest hair before his hands swept upward. His thumbs stroked beneath her breast once, twice, three times. Her nipples tight-ened painfully. She mashed her lips on a whimper.

Involuntarily, her head tipped back against him. He trailed kisses down her neck, across her shoulder and back to her jaw. She shouldn't be enjoying this. She didn't know him and wasn't certain she could trust him, but the rasp of his hands across her skin aroused her unbearably.

And then he covered her breasts. His fingers tweaked her nipples and something inside her detonated, radiating a delicious sensation from her core. A moan slipped between her teeth.

Franco murmured words in French as he caressed her, words she was too distracted to translate. Stacy squeezed her eyes shut and struggled to maintain control, to remember this was a business transaction, and then Franco's hand slipped into her panties and his fingers brushed over her most sensitive spot. Her thighs automatically clamped together against the intrusion, but Franco continued to stroke. He delved into her wetness and plied it over her flesh again and again. Circling. Tormenting. Tempting her to let go.

His foot nudged hers apart, opening her for deeper access, and his fingers plunged inside her. Her lungs emptied. Warmth expanded in her belly and her body trembled with need—need she fought to restrain. He pulled her hips flush against his. The length of his erection nudging the base of her spine fractured what little control she had maintained. And then suddenly the tension snapped and orgasm washed over her in waves of pulsing heat, buckling her knees and making her clutch Franco's arms to keep from falling to the floor. His caresses slowed, easing her though the aftershocks buffeting her.

So that's what all the fuss is about.

Winded and stunned by the intensity of her response, Stacy forced her lids open and met Franco's gaze in the mirror. Questions filled his eyes and her skin baked with embarrassment. Feeling raw and exposed, she ducked her head. He must think her totally shameless.

But then shameless is what he'd bought.

Five

Franco could not believe the evidence before him, but the wonder on Stacy's face and her current embarrassment could only have one cause. "Your first orgasm?"

She winced and dipped her chin in the slightest of nods.

Franco swiftly withdrew his hands. Not because her revelation repulsed him, but because her confession sent a volatile cocktail of emotions through him. Anger rose swiftly toward those who'd misused her, and possessiveness wasn't far behind. Stacy would be his, *certainement,* but only temporarily. The third and possibly the most dangerous reaction was understanding. Inexperience, not manipulation, explained the mixed signals she'd been sending him. None of those responses had any place in this relationship.

"Stacy." He waited until she eased open her eyes again. "Your first, but not your last."

Her lips parted and then relief replaced the surprise

in her eyes. Had she thought he would reject her because her past lovers had been selfish bastards? She might be a pawn in the game with his father, but she would not suffer for it.

He turned her in his arms and covered her mouth, gently this time. Seducing instead of taking. Sipping, suckling her bottom lip and teasing the silken inside with his tongue instead of ravaging her as he'd done earlier.

He still desired her, still hungered for her, but for her sake, he would dull the sharp edges of his need and make this good for her. Good for both of them. By the end of their month Stacy would be a sexually confident woman. She would not forget the lessons he taught her. That other men would benefit bothered him marginally, but he brushed the concern aside.

Inexperienced or not, she accepted your proposition. That makes her like all the others.

Stacy clutched his waist, bunching his shirt in her hands. He wanted her hands on his skin. He released her long enough to rip off the garment and cast it aside.

Stacy's breath caught. Her pupils expanded as her gaze explored his torso, following the line of hair to his waistband. He captured her hands and spread them over his skin and then glided their joined hands over his burning flesh. Her fingers threaded through his chest hair, tugging slightly, and sending electrifying bolts of pleasure straight to his groin. Her palms dragged across his nipples. His whistled indrawn breath mingled with her gasp as hunger charged through him. He released her hands and fisted his by his side, fighting the need to crush her to him.

She tentatively traced the lines defining his abdominal muscles, and his flesh contracted involuntarily beneath her curious fingers. His control wavered like tall trees in the hot sirocco winds.

What is this? You are no boy.

And yet he trembled like one.

"Unfasten my pants," he rasped.

She hesitated and then slipped her fingers between fabric and flesh. His stomach muscles clenched and his groin tightened as she fumbled the hook free and then reached for his zipper. Franco gritted his teeth as she lowered the tab over his erection.

Perhaps all women are born knowing how to torture a man.

When she finished the task, she paused, bit her lip and looked up at him though her thick lashes. His control frayed.

Franco moved out of reach, ripped back the covers and sat on the edge of the bed. He swiftly removed his shoes and socks, letting his gaze rove over her as he did so. Stacy did not have the stick-straight model figure to which so many women aspired these days. Her breasts were exquisite, round, the perfect size to fill his palms, and tipped with dusty-rose aureoles which he could not wait to taste. Her waist and hips curved nicely. Who would have guessed that she hid such an alluring body beneath her sedate clothing?

"Remove your panties." He didn't dare touch her. Not yet.

Her breath hitched and then her thumbs hooked into the black, shiny fabric and slowly pushed it over her hips and thighs to encircle her ankles. She toed them aside and crossed her hands in front of her dark curls. He shook his head. "Let me look at you. Next time I will taste you."

Her eyes closed. She swallowed.

Franco extended his hand. "Come."

Watching him warily, Stacy shuffled forward.

"Sit." She turned as if she were going to sit beside him on the bed, but he caught her, pulling her toward him until her legs straddled his. She slowly sank onto his thighs, her knees flanking his hips on the mattress and her buttocks resting on his lap. The position left her breasts level with his mouth and her feminine core open and exposed.

She was his, his to do with as he wanted, and at the moment he wanted her hot and wet and writhing with pleasure in his arms. He would wipe away the memory of her selfish lovers.

Franco pulled a nipple into his mouth, sucking, laving and gently nipping until her panted breaths stirred his hair. He caressed her back, her buttocks, savoring the smooth texture of her skin, the scent of her filling his lungs and the taste of her on his tongue. *"Touche-moi."*

She lifted her hands to his shoulders and then tangled her fingers in the hair at his nape.

He groaned against her breast. Need urged him to grind his hips against hers, but he settled for reaching between them to stroke her slick folds. Her short nails dug into his skin and a quiet whimper slipped free.

By the time he finished with her, she would not be shy about expressing her passion, he vowed.

His thumb found a rhythm to bring her satisfaction while he feasted on one nipple and then the other until she shuddered against his palm as *le petit mort* rippled over her. Not a moment too soon. Franco was about to erupt.

He stood abruptly, lifting her and then laying her on the bed. Just as he'd envisioned, only a passionate flush covered her skin. He swiftly removed his pants and briefs and reached into the bedside drawer for a condom. Lips parted and eyes wide, Stacy watched his every move as he donned protection. The color on her cheeks deepened and spread to her kiss-dampened breasts, and desire hammered insistently inside him.

He knelt between her legs, finesse and patience long gone, and cupped her buttocks in his hands. "Guide me inside, Stacy."

She curled her fingers around his length. He slammed his eyelids closed, clenched his teeth and stiffened his spine against the exquisite agony of her touch. She steered him toward her entrance and, muscles rigid and trembling with the effort to go slowly, Franco eased into her tight core one excruciating inch at a time. Restraint made his lungs burn and sweat bead on his skin.

When she lifted her hips to rush him the rest of the way in his control snapped. Franco surged deep, withdrew and plunged again and again and again. He fell forward, catching his weight on arms braced on the pillow beside her head. Stacy's back bowed, her arms encircled him, and her breasts teased his chest. The scrape of her nails on his back stimulated him past sanity. He gazed into her eyes and saw desire and surprise as her breath quickened and her body arched.

Her muffled cry as she climaxed again combined with the contracting of her inner muscles to hurdle him over the edge. His roar echoed off the walls as desire pulsed from him.

He collapsed to his elbows, satisfied and yet at the same time unsettled. Gasping for breath, he searched for the cause of his disquiet. And then understanding descended like a guillotine. Quick. Sharp. Cold.

He had let sex with Stacy become personal. A mistake he'd learned to avoid long ago.

It could not—would not—happen again.

* * *

Even before her pulse slowed, Stacy had regrets. What had she done? She'd had sex for money. And she'd enjoyed it.

What did that say about her?

Nothing complimentary, that's for sure.

She closed her eyes tightly and tried to distance herself from the lean, hard body of the man above her. *Inside her.* But she couldn't block out the comfortable weight of him pressing her into the mattress, his scent or the aroma of sex.

Franco rolled away to sit on the edge of the bed with his back curved and his elbows on his knees. Her sweat-dampened skin instantly chilled without the heating blanket of his body, but he was sitting on the covers. Feeling exposed and vulnerable, she crossed her ankles and hugged her arms over her breasts.

He rose and his pale backside mesmerized her. As much as she hated herself at the moment, the ashes inside her sparked to life at the sight of corded muscles rippling beneath the sleek, tanned skin as he shoved his fingers through his hair. The movement drew her gaze to the breadth of his shoulders. Had she made those scratches? Embarrassment flamed her face.

"Would you like to shower?" he asked in a flat, un-readable voice, without turning.

She blinked and looked away. "No. Thank you."

She wanted a shower. But not here. Not now. What if he decided to join her? He'd bought her. Did that mean she'd forfeited the right to say no? She hadn't yet come to terms with the pleasure he'd wrung from her tonight, so she wasn't ready for another intimate encounter. She had to keep this affair impersonal, because opening up to more than that would make her vulnerable.

But there had been nothing impersonal in what they'd just shared. At least not on her part.

Sex for money. She clutched the thought close—like a talisman. As ugly as it sounded, it was safer than trusting her heart to a man like Franco Constantine. A man with more money and probably more power than her father.

The moment he disappeared into the bathroom Stacy vaulted from the bed and snatched up her clothing. Her hands trembled so badly it took three tries to fasten her bra. In her haste she pulled her panties on wrong-side out, but she didn't dare take time to remove them and put them on again. She wanted to be dressed before Franco returned. Dressed and ready to leave.

She stumbled over her shoes—she couldn't even remember removing them—and shoved her feet inside, and then snatched up her dress and dragged it over her head. The zipper stuck in the middle of her back. Frustrated tears stung her eyes as she tugged in vain. She bit her lip, blinked furiously and willed them away.

Gentle hands nudged hers aside. Stacy nearly jumped out of her pumps. She hadn't heard Franco return. His knuckles brushed against her spine, raising goose bumps as he fiddled with the zipper, freed the fabric and pulled up the tab.

Stacy stiffened her resolve and met his gaze in the mirror. His broader naked form framed hers. Her hair was a mess and her lips were swollen, but she didn't care. "I want to go back to the hotel."

His jaw shifted. All signs of passion had vanished from his face, leaving his features hard and drawn. "I'll drive you."

"I'll wait in the living room." She bolted.

"Stacy." His voice halted her on the threshold.

Reluctantly, she turned. Her breath caught at the sight of Franco in all his naked glory standing with one knee cocked and his torso slightly angled in her direction. The man had a body worthy of the beefcake calendar someone had given Candace at her bridal shower. His chest was wide and covered with dark curls, the muscles clearly defined, but not bulky like a body builder's. A line of hair led to a denser, darker crop surrounding a masculine package any centerfold would be proud to claim, and his legs were long and strong.

"Are you all right?" The question seemed forced.

Physically? "Yes."

Mentally? She was a wreck. She'd never felt more alone or confused or ashamed of herself. She needed to reassess. Maybe financial security wasn't worth it. On the other hand, she'd enjoyed sex for the first time in her life. But sex with a man she'd known only three days. Brazen, that's what she'd been.

"I will be with you in a few moments," Franco said, reaching for his shirt.

Stacy nodded and fled. Agitated and anxious, she paced the length of the living room, skirting the red rugs and ending at the kitchen archway. She needed to do something to channel her thoughts and nervous energy. Her gaze lit upon the dirty dishes. Seconds later she had them submerged in a sink filled with hot soapy water. She scrubbed the fine china probably harder than she should have.

Franco had turned cold immediately after he'd…finished. Had she turned him off with her fumbling and inexperience? What if he drove her to the hotel and told her to forget the deal? At this moment she wasn't sure that wouldn't be a good thing. She wasn't sure about anything except that she needed to be alone.

She cleaned the second plate, rinsed and dried it and then tackled the stemware.

"Que fais-tu?" Franco asked from behind her, startling her into almost dropping the last glass.

She didn't turn. "I'm washing the dishes."

"My housekeeper comes tomorrow."

She finished drying the wineglass, set it on the counter and carefully folded the damp towel, delaying facing him until the last possible moment. When she did she focused on the cleft in his chin rather than his eyes. "It's done."

"You are my mistress, Stacy, not my maid."

Mistress. Her mother would have been appalled. Her mother, who'd always told Stacy the right man would treat her like a princess. Her mother, who'd led a secret life Stacy hadn't known about until the investigation into her mother's murder had revealed details of a life that looked like a fairy tale to outsiders, but had actually been a nightmare.

"Am I? Still?"

Franco closed the distance between them. He'd dressed in the clothing he'd worn earlier, but without the tie or jacket, and he'd left the top few buttons of his shirt open. Her traitorous nipples tightened at the memory of those dark, wiry curls teasing her breasts.

He reached out and lifted her chin, forcing Stacy to look into his eyes—eyes that no longer burned with passion, but were completely inscrutable instead. "Unless you find my touch repugnant, and I don't think you do, *mon gardénia,* then our agreement stands."

She couldn't speak and didn't know what she'd say if she could find her voice. Did she want the affair to continue? His fingers stroked down her neck, making her pulse leap and her skin tingle. Apparently, no matter what her brain said, her body was all for the affair.

He withdrew his hand. "Come. I'll drive you to the hotel."

"You look shell-shocked."

Stacy pivoted and found Madeline behind her in the hotel lobby. "Hi."

"Was that Franco I saw leaving?"

"Yes." After a silent ride from his home, Franco had insisted on walking her inside. Stacy hadn't invited him upstairs.

"Okay, Stace, what gives?"

"Nothing. I…we had dinner." He hadn't kissed her goodnight, and she didn't know whether that was good or bad.

"Uh-huh, and what else?"

Her cheeks burned. She wished she and Madeline were closer, because she needed to talk to someone, and she was certain the more experienced woman would be able to help her unravel her tangled and conflicting emotions.

"Stacy, did he hurt you?"

"No, no, it's nothing like that. We should go up. It's late."

"It's barely midnight, and we're not going upstairs until you tell me what has you fluctuating between blood-red and hospital-sheet white." Madeline hooked her arm through Stacy's and half led, half dragged her toward the bar.

Within minutes Madeline had snagged them a secluded table, an attentive waiter and a couple of fruity cocktails. "Drink and spill."

Stacy didn't know where to begin or how much to share with this woman whom she'd only met a week ago.

"Okay, let me start. You slept with him and…" Madeline prodded.

Stacy choked on her drink. "How did you know?"

Madeline shrugged. "Was it good? Because I'm going to be seriously disappointed if a guy as sexy as Franco Constantine was a lousy lay."

Lousy lay. The words echoed in Stacy's head, an unpleasant blast from the past, compliments of the high-school jock who'd wooed her until she'd surrendered her virginity. She'd thought being a popular guy's girlfriend would win her acceptance in a new school, but afterward he'd dumped her and told all his friends she was a lousy lay. That was the first time Stacy had welcomed her mother's decision to relocate.

Madeline gripped her hand. "You've gone pale again. Start talking, Stace, or I'm calling the cops, because I'm starting to think he forced you do something you didn't want to do."

"No, don't. There's no need for that. Yes, we slept together and no, it wasn't lousy. He didn't hurt me or force me. I promise." Uncomfortable with the confession, she shifted in her seat.

"Did he dump you?"

"No."

"Then what's the problem?"

She hesitated and then confessed in a whisper, "I barely know him and I had sex with him."

"So?"

So she felt like a tramp. Worse, she'd made a bargain with a man who had the power to make her repeat her mother's mistakes. Not one of her finest decisions.

"You weren't a virgin, were you?"

"No."

"Then I'm not seeing a problem. It was good, right?"

Stacy could feel a blush climbing her neck as she nodded.

"And what's wrong with being with a guy who makes you feel good as long as he's not diseased, married or committed to someone else?"

Stacy fidgeted with her napkin. "Nothing, I guess."

"Stace, there are plenty of guys out there who'll make you feel like crap. You have to grab the good ones when you can. And if it lasts, great. If it doesn't…well, you tried. As long as you're careful. STDs are ugly. Take my word on that. I see plenty of them in the E.R."

Madeline took a sip of her drink and then continued, "It's a double standard, you know? Guys are expected to be experienced and good in bed, but women are supposed to virtuously wait for Mr. Right. How will we recognize him if we don't look around? And what happens when our Mr. Right turns out to be a total jerk?"

Stacy vaguely remembered Candace mentioning a nasty breakup in Madeline's past. She tentatively covered Madeline's hand offering support, but at the same time Madeline's words lifted a load from Stacy's shoulders.

An affair with Franco wouldn't hurt anyone as long as she remembered his passion-profit-and-no-promises offer was temporary and kept her heart safely sealed off. For the first time all night she smiled. "Thanks, Madeline. I needed to hear that."

"Hey, that's what friends are for."

Friends. Stacy savored the word and nodded.

When she left Monaco behind she'd have friends, good memories of sex instead of only bad ones, and for the first time in her life, she'd have a nest egg and soon, a home of her own.

And she'd be an ocean away from the man who threatened her equilibrium.

"Everybody needs to take a nap today," Candace said as she entered the sitting room for breakfast and their usual planning session Friday morning. She placed her cell phone on the coffee table. Candace was the only one of the women who had one that worked in Monaco. Their U.S. cell phones were useless here.

"Why?" Stacy asked.

"Because Franco's taking us to Jimmy'z tonight. He says the place doesn't start rocking until after midnight."

Franco. Stacy's heart skipped a beat. She'd wondered when she'd see him again. Wednesday night he'd left her with a vague, "I will be in touch."

Because she refused to waste a day in paradise sitting in her room and waiting for him to call, she'd spent yesterday exploring Monaco-Ville, the oldest section of Monaco, alone. Her suitemates had other commitments. She'd looked over her shoulder countless times as she watched the changing of the palace guard, wondering if she'd run into Franco, but he'd have no reason to visit tourist spots like the Prince's Palace or the wax museum. He'd probably seen it all before. Besides, he was probably at his office…wherever that was.

Filled with a mixture of anticipation and dread, she'd returned to the hotel late in the afternoon. But there'd been no message from Franco. Stacy had shared a quiet meal at a sidewalk café with Candace and then gone to bed early, only to toss and turn all night.

How could she miss a man she didn't even know? She blamed her uneasiness on not wanting to violate the terms of their agreement by being unavailable. It definitely wasn't a desire to see him again. The warmth between her thighs called her a liar.

"Typical of a guy," Candace continued, "he was stumped when I asked him what we should wear."

Stacy reached for one of her three guide books, looked up the club and read aloud, "'Jimmy'z—An exclusive dance club where the jet set hangs out. Dress code—casual to formal, but wear your designer labels.'"

Stacy didn't own any designer labels.

"You three can go shopping after we tour the Oceanographic Museum and the cathedral this morning," Candace said. "But I have an appointment with the stylist for a practice session on my wedding-day hairdo."

Madeline shook her head. "Not me. I have plans for later."

"Same here," Amelia offered.

Stacy couldn't afford anything new, and she refused to let Candace keep buying things for her. "I'll find something in my closet."

And just like that Franco undermined Stacy's concentration for a second day. Every tall, dark-haired man she spotted in the distance Friday morning made her pulse spike, and no matter how impressive the sights, she kept thinking about Franco and the night ahead. Had it not been for her lack of sleep for the past three nights she wouldn't have been dead to the world when the suite doorbell rang later that afternoon. Shoving her hair out of her eyes she stumbled groggily into the sitting room, opened the door to a hotel staff member.

"A package for Ms. Reeves," he said.

"I'm Stacy Reeves." She accepted the large rectangular pewter-colored box and the man turned away. "Wait. I'll get a tip."

"It's been taken care of, mademoiselle. *Bonsoir.*"

He turned away. Stacy closed the door and leaned against it, her exhaustion totally eradicated. Only Franco would send her something. She pushed off the door and carried the package into her room. With trembling hands she plucked at the lavender ribbon and opened the box.

A folded piece of ivory stationery lay on top of the lavender tissue paper. She lifted it and read, For tonight.

No name. No signature. But the handwriting was the same as that on the card included with Franco's flowers. Franco. She inhaled a shaky breath and pushed back the tissue paper to reveal a pile of teal garments, the same shade as the Mediterranean Sea outside the hotel windows.

She pulled out the first piece, a soft, silk camisole, and laid it on the bed. The second, a sheer, beaded wrap top, matched perfectly, as did the third, a handkerchief-hem skirt with the same beading on the edges as the wrap. She held the skirt against her body. It would be fitted from her waist through her hips, but the lower half would swish and swirl about her thighs as she moved. The perfect dancing outfit, and judging by the designer label, it probably cost more than her monthly rent and car payment combined.

And then her gaze caught on two more wrapped items in the bottom of the box. She unwound the tissue from the largest first and found strappy sandals to match the clothing. She slipped one on her bare foot. Perfect fit. In fact, everything looked as if it would fit. How had Franco known her sizes? Even she didn't know the European conversions. Had Candace told him? Or was he so experienced with women he could accurately guess their sizes just by looking at them. Probably the latter.

She opened the last package, gasped and dropped the

matching bra and thong in the exact same shade of teal on the bed. Heat rushed through her.

Franco was dressing her from the skin out. He'd bought the privilege to do so, just as he'd bought the right to undress her later if he chose.

Anticipation—or was it dread?—made her pulse race.

Six

A wiser man would choose another woman, Franco told himself as he entered Hôtel Reynard a few minutes before midnight. Stacy had made him feel more than sexual relief—a luxury he no longer afforded himself. It would not happen again.

He had ignored her yesterday just to prove he could, but he had failed miserably. She had invaded his thoughts like a fever. If the family estate and the company he had sweated blood over were not at stake, he would bid her farewell. But it had taken him two months after making the agreement with his father to find a woman who met both his and his father's criteria. Stacy came with the added benefit of leaving the country after the month was up. He would not have to deal with a clingy woman who refused to accept goodbye.

Nodding to the concierge, Franco stepped into the penthouse elevator and swiftly ascended. Tonight there would be no intimate conversations. He would dance with Stacy in the crowded, noisy club. Afterward he would send her suitemates back to the hotel in the limo and take Stacy to his villa where they would have sex. And then he would put her in a cab and send her back to the hotel. Alone.

He did not want to know her better—except intimately, of course. Nor did he want to discover what had made an attractive and intelligent woman completely unaware of her appeal, for she seemed to have absolutely no vanity.

The suite's doorbell chimed when he touched the button, and seconds later the wooden panel swung open. Stacy. She took his breath away. His gaze absorbed her, from her loose shining hair to the outfit he had chosen, down her lovely legs to her pink-painted toenails in the sexy heels.

"Tu es ravissante, mon gardénia," he murmured in a barely audible—thanks to the annoying thickening of this throat—voice.

Her cheeks pinked and she dipped her chin. "Thank you. And if I look ravishing it's because of the lovely outfit. Thank you for that too. But you don't have to buy—"

"The color matches your eyes when you climax," he interrupted. Ignoring her shocked gasp, he reached for her right hand and bent to kiss her knuckles. At the same time he retrieved the diamond bracelet she had left behind from his pocket and fastened it on her wrist.

He straightened. "Are your suitemates ready? I have a limo downstairs."

"Is that Franco?" Candace called from within the suite.

Fingering the bracelet, Stacy stepped back, opening the door and revealing the trio of women. "Yes. He has a limo waiting."

"Then let's go," Madeline replied. "And Stace, if that's the kind of stuff you have stashed in your closet I'm glad we're the same size."

Stacy shot him a quick glance as if warning him not to correct Madeline. "I need to get my purse."

His gaze followed her as she walked away, the uneven hem of her skirt swinging flirtatiously above her knees. Knowing her buttocks were bare save the clinging fabric of her skirt and the thin ribbon of her thong made his blood pool behind his zipper. Nor could he take his eyes from her once she rejoined them. This fascination was not good. But it was temporary. He would get over it.

In the limo he settled beside her with the other women on the seat across from them. Stacy's scent filled his nostrils and her legs drew his gaze. His fisted his hand against the compulsion to smooth his palm up her thigh.

He belatedly remembered the role Vincent had asked of him. "I have a table reserved beside the dance floor. The rules are different here than in the States. Unattached men and women dance freely without partners. If you see someone you wish to dance with you make eye contact, and if the interest is returned you move toward each other on the floor."

"You mean the guys don't ask you to dance?" Amelia queried.

"Not verbally, no. The club is safe, but if you have problems come to me. Stacy and I will be nearby."

Stacy's eyes widened. She seemed to sink deeper into the seat as her companions' speculative gazes landed on her. She had not wanted her friends to know about the money, but hiding the affair would be impossible.

Franco nodded to Candace. "Vincent says you are only to dance with women or ugly men."

His comment brought a laugh and eased the tension. "The limo is on standby. If you wish to leave, use it. Don't get into cars with strangers."

A collective groan arose from the opposite bench and Madeline mumbled, "Not my father's favorite speech."

Franco shrugged. "Vincent charged me with your safety."

The limo pulled to a stop outside Jimmy'z. The women climbed out, Stacy last. Franco followed, his gaze on her shapely bottom. The men gathered near the entrance eyed the women, Stacy in particular. Franco rested a possessive hand on her waist and bent closer. "You will dance with no one but me."

She briefly closed her eyes and then nodded.

Inside, the hostess led them to their table. The club was dark and the music loud with a driving beat. Franco wondered what Stacy thought of the retro decor, but decided it did not matter. Knowing her tastes was not part of their deal.

He arranged for their drinks and waited with impatience he had no business feeling for Stacy to consume hers while the women chatted, pointed out celebrities and acclimatized themselves to the club. An hour later even the shy Amelia had deserted them for the dance floor. Franco extended his hand. Stacy bit her lip, hesitating before she laid her palm over his and rose.

Thankful that slow songs were few and far between at Jimmy'z, he led her onto the floor. The night would be long enough without the arousing slide of her body against his. Needing the physical exertion to expend some of his caged energy, he released her hand and found the rhythm of the beat. Stacy moved self-consciously at first, but soon either the gyrating crowd surrounding them or the alcohol relaxed her. The results devastated him. A slight sheen of sweat dampened her flushed skin, reminding him of her face just before *le petit mort*. He would have been better off if Stacy had remained stiff.

His gaze slid over her. When he had chosen her clothing he'd had no idea the effect she would have on his control and his carefully planned evening. Each pirouette flared her skirt almost to her bottom. He wasn't the only man to notice. A primitive urge to mark her as his surged through him.

He cupped a hand around her nape, pulled her close and pressed a quick, hard kiss on her lips. He said into her ear, "You dance like you make love. *Très* sexy."

Shock made Stacy stumble. Could the man read minds? Franco caught her quickly, pulling her flush against the hot length of his hard body. The contact was too intense, too arousing. She jerked back, her gaze slamming into his. Suddenly the air seemed loaded with sexual tension.

For the past two hours she'd been thinking he moved like an invitation to sin—an invitation she wanted to accept more and more with each passing second. She'd believed that after a night in his bed she couldn't—wouldn't—desire him again. Wrong. Her body, already warm from dancing, flushed with heat and pulsed with a sexual awareness with which she'd been unfamiliar until Franco.

Franco moved closer, his hand curving around her waist and his hips punctuating the beat in a purely sensual dance that made her feminine muscles clench in anticipation. A mating dance. Not graphic or crude. Just devastatingly, pulse-acceleratingly sensuous. And she wasn't the only woman to notice. Since they'd arrived, each time Stacy had glanced past the cobalt silk stretched across his broad shoulders she'd caught women glaring at her or ogling Franco's behind, and who could blame them?

More than one bold woman had sashayed up to them on the dance floor and shimmied directly beside him as if trying to draw his attention. But Franco's gaze never strayed. His eyes had remained locked on hers or on the movement of her body with an intensity burning in the blue depths that made her feel incredibly attractive and yes, very desirable. Realizing she was proud to be the woman he'd chosen was a scary thought since the man *should* be her worst nightmare.

Her throat dried and her belly tightened. She blamed the discomforts on thirst and hunger. Nerves over this evening had ruined her appetite and she'd barely touched the dinner she and her suitemates had shared earlier. Hoping for a distraction, she dampened her lips and glanced toward their table, but her friends weren't there to rescue her.

Franco intercepted her look, caught her hand and led her off the dance floor without a word. He paused beside her chair, brushed stray tendrils of hair from her damp forehead and tucked them behind her ears. His fingertips lingered over her pulse points, no doubt noting the rapid tattoo not solely caused by the dancing, and then one hand traced her collar bone and dipped into the V of her top. Desire rippled over her, tightening her nipples and making her shiver.

"Another drink, *mon gardénia?*"

Maybe the alcohol was to blame for loosening her inhibitions and erasing her common sense. Whatever, she wanted him to kiss her instead of staring at her lips as if he would consume her were they not surrounded by people, and her response was both unacceptable and unwise, given what she knew of men in his position.

She cleared her throat and sat. "Water this time."

He signaled the waiter, ordered another round of drinks for their table and seated himself beside her.

Stacy gasped when his hand smoothed up from her knee and then her breath wheezed out again when his fingertips stroked along the sensitive skin of her inner thigh.

"You wish to go?"

She did. Oh boy, she did. What did it say about her that she couldn't wait to get back to his house, back to his bed? She waited until after the waiter deposited the drinks and left to reply. "We shouldn't leave before the others."

"Amelia has found someone. Madeline and Candace are coming this way."

Surprised that he'd kept track of her suitemates, she turned in her seat and searched the crowd until she located Amelia dancing with a tall, sandy-haired man. "Should we leave her with him?"

"Toby will take care of her."

"Toby? Toby Haynes? The race-car driver?"

"*Oui,* and Vincent's best man. He is also charged with your safety while you are in Monaco." He removed his hand as the women neared the table and Stacy immediately missed his touch.

Something is definitely wrong with you.

Madeline and Candace slid into their seats.

"*Merci,* Franco," Candace said. She and Madeline toasted him with their fresh drinks. "This has been a blast, but I wish Vincent were here."

Madeline scanned the crowd. "And Damon. I had hoped he'd join us tonight."

"Damon is your tour guide?" Stacy asked.

"Yes. But I guess he had to work tonight."

"Shall I call for the limo for you?" Franco asked.

"Yes," Madeline and Candace answered simultaneously.

"Excuse me." Franco left the table, headed onto the dance floor and spoke to Toby and then disappeared toward the club entrance.

Candace grinned mischievously. "I'll tell ya, Stacy, Franco is definitely a keeper. He has some seriously sexy moves, and if he's half as good in bed as he is on the dance floor, a girl could have a real good time."

Stacy's cheeks burned. She ducked her head and fiddled with her cocktail napkin. So this was girl talk. "He's a good, um…dancer."

"You're going home with him?" Madeline asked.

Stacy fought the urge to squirm in her seat. "Yes, but I'll be back for our morning meeting."

"The only thing on the agenda tomorrow is me tinkering with the rehearsal dinner and reception seating. No work for you, so stay as long as you like," Candace replied with a wink and a smug smile. "It's almost 3:00 a.m. I have a feeling we'll all be sleeping in."

Stacy had permission to spend the entire night with Franco. Did she want to? The swiftness of her answer surprised and alarmed her. She'd slid far too easily into the role of a rich man's mistress.

"Remove your clothing," Franco ordered in the darkness thirty minutes later.

Stacy's breath caught. She couldn't see anything, not even her hand in front of her face, and she didn't know where she was. Franco had led her into his home, and without turning on any lights, he'd guided her down a hall and a flight of stairs.

The click of her heels had echoed off the walls until

they'd stopped moving and now the eerie silence deafened her. Or maybe her thunderous heartbeat drowned out all sound.

Did she dare trust him? She found herself wanting to. Scary.

A mechanical whirl startled her, making her look to her right. The wall slid open like a curtain to reveal moon-washed gardens, the roar of a waterfall and a spa large enough to lie down in without touching the sides.

Half of the spa is concealed beneath the house by the falling water. I would like to make love to you there, Franco had said. Was it only a day and a half ago?

A thrill of anticipation raced through her. Anticipation. Something she'd never experienced in a relationship with a man before Franco.

Moonlight seeped around the cascading water to dimly illuminate her surroundings, and a gentle breeze wafted in, carrying the scent of flowers. The people of Monaco loved their flowers. Gardens and flower boxes abounded.

Stacy scanned the room filled with more exercise equipment than the gym in her apartment complex until she spotted Franco in the shadows. He flipped a switch and the whirlpool splashed to life, its water gleaming like bubbly champagne from the golden glow of lights beneath the surface.

With his gaze fixed on her he leaned against the wall, toed off his shoes and removed his socks. Mesmerized, she watched as he straightened and reached for the buttons on his shirt. It fluttered to the floor followed quickly by his pants and briefs. He stood before her like a finely chiseled statue. An incredibly aroused and well-endowed statue. His chin lifted. "Your turn."

She gulped and reached for the knot of her sheer wrap, but she was nervous, her fingers uncooperative.

She'd never stripped for a man before. Nor had she ever had one look at her the way Franco did with his gaze burning over her, his nostrils flaring, his fists clenched by his side. Finally, the knot gave way. She shrugged off the wrap and dropped it on a nearby weight bench.

Taking a fortifying breath, she reached for the back hook and zipper of her skirt. It swished down her legs. She stepped out of it and her shoes and turned to deposit both on the bench.

A warm hand covered her bottom, making her jump and gasp. Franco. She hadn't heard him cross the room. His other hand joined the first, stroking her buttocks, thighs and her belly, and molding her against him. The thong was no barrier to the heat of his lean flanks against her cheeks and the hard length of his erection against her spine. Desire made her dizzy.

What happened to maintaining a clear head and control?

He murmured something in French, something she couldn't translate, and then his fingers caught the hem of her camisole and whisked it over her head.

"Turn around," he ordered in a deep, velvety voice.

She pivoted on trembling legs. The sharp rasp of his indrawn breath filled her ears. He lifted a hand to outline the top of her demi-bra with a fingertip. Her nipples tightened and need twisted inside her as he retraced his path, this time delving below the lace and over her sensitive skin. How could he make her want like this?

"Take it off."

Stacy reached behind her, unhooked the bra and shrugged out of it. Franco's approving gaze caressed her breasts and then dropped to the tiny teal thong.

"And the rest."

She shoved the lingerie down her legs wondering

why she had not once considered saying no. And then she straightened. Franco tipped his head to indicate the spa. Stacy descended the whirlpool steps. The hot water swirled around her ankles, her calves, and once she reached the center of the small pool, her thighs. Franco joined her, reclined on the bench seat and extended his hand.

"Turn around."

She did and then he pulled her into his lap and flattened her back against his chest with his erection sandwiched in the crease of her buttocks. The water swirled between her legs and lapped at her breasts, but then Franco's caressing hands replaced it, massaging, tweaking, sweeping her up in a whirlpool of desire.

She let him have his way. He'd bought her, bought the right to use her any way he wanted. And she had to remember that, but it was hard to keep up the mental barriers when he touched her like this. Sure, he'd promised her pleasure, but did she really deserve it?

His teeth grazed the tendons of her neck. She shivered and tilted her head to give him better access. He stroked her breasts, her abdomen, her legs, nearing but never quite reaching the place where she needed his touch the most. She squirmed in his lap and bit back a frustrated whimper. He stood abruptly, lifting her with him, sat her on the cool tile edge of the whirlpool and then knelt between her legs.

Next time I will taste you, he'd said.

"Wait—" The touch of his tongue cut off her shocked protest with an intense burst of sensation. No man had ever licked her there. Franco laved and suckled, taking her to the brink again and again, but each time she thought she'd shatter he'd stop to kiss her thigh, nibble her hip bone or tongue her navel.

Frustration built until she unclenched her fingers from the rim of the tub and tangled them in his hair to hold him in place.

He grunted a satisfied sound against her and then found the heart of her again with his silken tongue. Seconds later climax undulated through her. Her cries echoed off the stone walls and her muscles contracted over and over, squeezing every last drop of energy from her until she sagged against Franco's bent head and braced her arms on his broad shoulders.

He straightened, reached behind her for a condom packet she hadn't even noticed and quickly readied himself. Cupping her bottom, he pulled her to the edge of the spa and plunged deep inside her, forcing another lusty cry from her lungs. She shoved her fist against her mouth.

Franco pulled her hand away. "I want to hear the sound of your passion. Better yet, I want to taste your cries on my tongue."

He covered her mouth with his.

She ought to be ashamed of herself, Stacy thought as she clung to him and arched to meet his thrusts, but she couldn't seem to rally the emotion with Franco pistoning into her core and bringing her to the brink of another climax. She yanked her mouth free and gasped for breath as her muscles tensed and she came again, this time calling out his name.

Franco plunged harder, deeper and faster until he roared in release, and then all was silent except for the rush of the water and their panting breaths.

He held her, or maybe she held him, as he sank back into the hot water, taking her boneless body with him. She drifted above him. The current swirled over her sensitized skin, teasing, tantalizing, slowing her return to sanity. Without Franco's arms to anchor her, she'd float away like a cork on the tide. She trusted him to keep her head above water.

Trust. The thought jarred her into planting her knees on the bottom of the tub on either side of Franco's hips and pushing him away so abruptly that she almost dunked him. How could she trust him? He was everything she'd sworn to avoid, but avoiding him was becoming the last thing she wanted to do.

To protect herself she'd have to learn everything she could about him. Did he have a temper? Any obsessions?

She'd learn—even if learning meant letting her guard down enough to spend the night.

"I'll call a taxi for you." Franco disentangled their bodies and stood. He stepped over the low wall separating the indoor and outdoor halves of the spa and ducked beneath the waterfall. The cooler water from the pool sheeted down on his head and splashed over Stacy's skin. Seconds later he climbed from the whirlpool.

Stacy rose on legs so rubbery it was a miracle they supported her, and wrapped her arms around her waist. "Candace said there's nothing on the agenda for tomorrow—today. I—I can stay."

Muscles rippling beneath his wet skin, he disappeared into an adjoining room without responding and returned moments later with a black towel around his hips and another in his fist. When she didn't take it from his outstretched arm he dropped it beside the spa. "I have other plans for the weekend."

Plans? With another woman? Stacy didn't care to identify the uncomfortable emotions stirring inside her. She had no claim on Franco's time. In fact, she should be glad he wanted to spend it elsewhere. But strangely, she wasn't.

"There is a change of clothing for you in the bathroom." A tilt of his head indicated the room he'd just vacated. He flicked a series of switches. The wall slid closed, the whirlpool stilled and silence and darkness descended on the room. Then overhead lights flashed on leaving Stacy feeling naked and exposed under his thorough perusal. Her damp skin quickly chilled.

"You may shower, if you like, and then join me upstairs." He gathered his discarded garments and left.

Dismissed. He'd had his way with her and now he was done. How could he be so conscientious of her satisfaction one moment and then such a cold bastard the next? Shame crept over her.

What are you doing? Falling for the first guy to give you an orgasm? So he's a good lover. He bought *you. Just because he's doing favors for Vincent and he watched out for your friends at the club doesn't make him a nice guy.*

And he has plans. *Plans that don't include you.*

Irritated with herself, Stacy climbed from the water, dried off and wound the towel around her nakedness. She grabbed her shoes and clothing from the weight bench and let curiosity lead her into a humongous tiled bathroom. A large glass shower stall took up one corner and a wooden sauna occupied the other. And was that a massage table? Did Franco have a personal masseuse?

A V-neck sundress in a muted floral print of blues and greens and a matching lightweight sweater hung in an open closet beside a white toweling robe. She ran her fingers over the dress's flirty ruffled hem. Silk, whereas her dresses were cotton. Designer instead of department store. Other than the sexy but impractical sandals in a box on the floor of the closet, the outfit was exactly the style she would have chosen for herself if she had an unlimited budget. Which, of course, she'd never had.

The dress tempted her, but she didn't want anything else from Franco, nor did she want to explain to her suitemates why he kept buying her presents.

Her reflection in the long mirror caught her eye. Ugh. Her makeup was ninety percent gone and her hair clumped in wet tangles over her shoulders. She dumped her clothes on the counter, washed her face in the sink and then finger-combed her hair as best as she could. She unhooked the diamond bracelet and left it on the long marble vanity and froze. Her heart stalled. *Her watch.* She hadn't removed it. Panic dried her mouth. Where had she misplaced it?

She backtracked, but didn't see it on the bottom of the spa or anywhere around the weight bench. It hadn't been expensive, but its value couldn't be measured in dollars. She remembered putting it on tonight. Wherever it was, she *had* to find it.

Maybe Franco could help. She returned to the bathroom and quickly yanked on her dancing outfit. The cool, sweat-dampened fabric made her grimace. After smoothing the wrinkles with her hands, she followed the direction Franco had taken earlier. The stairs led to a hallway, and while she would have preferred to explore this end of the house and perhaps learn more about Franco, she tracked his voice to the living room. With his back to her, he swore, dropped the phone on the cradle and shoved his hands through his damp dark hair.

"Is something wrong?"

He turned, his gaze narrowing over her choice of clothing. He'd changed into jeans and a black polo shirt. "The taxi is unavailable for an hour. I will drive you back to the hotel. Why are you not wearing the dress?"

"I told you. You don't have to keep buying me gifts. I accepted this one because I didn't have anything suitable to wear tonight, but otherwise…" She shrugged. "I don't need anything."

His lips compressed and a muscle in his jaw jumped. "And the bracelet?"

"I left it downstairs on the counter. It's beautiful, but not practical for an accountant. If I wore it to work people would wonder if I'd been embezzling from their accounts, and I never go anywhere dressy enough to need something like that."

Surprise flicked in his eyes. "You will continue to work when you return home?"

"Of course." As soon as she found another job. "Once I pay taxes on the money and buy a house there won't be enough left to live a life of idle luxury."

"Taxes? And what job will you list as a source for your income?"

Good question. She twisted the thin gold strap of her evening bag. "I haven't figured that out yet, but suddenly opening a bank account with more than a million dollars would red-flag the IRS. And I'm not stupid enough to keep that much cash lying around my apartment."

"Why not use an offshore bank?"

"Too cloak-and-dagger. I'd feel like a money launderer. Besides, not reporting the income would be illegal." Did he think she was crazy not to hide the money? She couldn't tell from his neutral expression. "Franco, I lost my watch. I didn't see it downstairs. Could you give me the number for the limo service, the taxi and Jimmy'z? I'll call to see if anyone found it. It wasn't expensive, but it was…my favorite. I need to find it."

"I will make the calls."

"Thank you." She agreed because the language barrier might be an issue, but then shifted in her sandals, reluctant for some stupid reason to see the night end. "I enjoyed tonight."

He folded his arms and leaned his hips against the back of the sofa. "You sound surprised."

She rubbed her bare wrist and wrinkled her nose. "I'm not a clubbing kind of person."

He studied her so intently her toes curled in her shoes, and then he reached behind him and lifted a small plastic shopping bag. "This is one gift I insist you accept. A cell phone. My numbers are already programmed into it."

She'd be at his beck and call. But that's what he'd bought. And the phone might come in handy when she needed to reach Candace or if one of the women needed to reach her. "Am I allowed to use it to call anyone else?"

"Not your lover in the States," he replied swiftly.

She took the bag from him and peeked inside to see a top-of-the-line silvery-green picture phone. "I meant Candace, Madeline or Amelia. I don't have a lover back home. If I did, I wouldn't be involved with you."

Again he looked as if he didn't believe what she said—a circumstance she was beginning to get used to. He pushed off the sofa. "Come."

She followed him outside and slid into the passenger seat of his car and waited until he climbed in beside her. "Why did you choose MIT?"

He didn't answer until he'd buckled his seat belt and started the engine. "They have an excellent Global Leadership program."

"Couldn't you get that at a university closer to home?"

He pulled onto the road and drove perhaps a half mile before replying. "My mother was from Boston and I was curious about her city."

Stacy jerked in surprise. "An American?"

Another long pause suggested he didn't want to share personal info. "Second-generation. She met my father while visiting her cousin in Avignon."

The lights of Monaco sparkled across the mountainside in the pre-dawn hour. Stacy didn't think she'd ever tire of the view, but the insights into Franco fascinated her more. "Are you close to her? Your mom, I mean."

"She died when I was three," the brusque response seemed grudgingly offered.

"I'm sorry. It's hard to lose a parent." She still missed hers, and now that she knew why she and her mother had lived such a vagabond life, she could even accept, respect and forgive her mother's choices.

A streetlight briefly illuminated his tense face. "Yours?"

A gruesome graphic image flashed through Stacy's mind. She squeezed her eyes shut and forced it away. "She…died when I was nineteen."

"And she left you enough money to attend college?"

"No. I co-oped."

"What is that?"

"I worked part-time in my field with sponsoring companies and that meant I had to take a lighter load of classes. It took six years of going to school year-round, but I finished."

"Vincent did not tell me that."

"You asked Vincent about me? What did he say?"

"That he had not met you, but that you had…how did he put it? You saved Candace's bacon in a tax audit."

Stacy laughed and Franco's gaze whipped in her direction. He acted as if he'd never heard her laugh. Come to think of it, he probably hadn't. "Candace's was my first audit, and I went a little overboard in her defense. I think the IRS agent was glad to get rid of us by the time

I finished pointing out all the deductions Candace could have taken but hadn't."

Franco pulled the car into the hotel parking area, but not into the valet lane and stopped. He turned in his seat and studied her face in the dim light. "You enjoy your work."

"I love—um, my job." She'd barely caught herself before using past tense. Being laid off had been like moving to a new school and being rejected all over again. It had hurt—especially since she hadn't done anything wrong. "Numbers make sense. People often don't."

He pinned her with another one of his intense inspections that made her want to squirm. "I will be out of town this weekend. A car will pick you up at quarter to six Monday evening and deliver you to my house. My housekeeper will let you in before she leaves. Wait for me. We will have dinner."

And then sex? Her shameless pulse quickened. "I look forward to it."

And the sad thing was, that wasn't a lie, and Monday seemed a very long way away.

Seven

"I have found her," Franco said upon entering the chateau's study.

His father looked up sharply, set his book aside and rose from the sofa to embrace him. "Franco, I was not expecting you this weekend. If you had called I could have delayed lunch."

He hadn't known he was coming. This morning's urge to put some distance between him and Stacy had been both sudden and imperative. She had clouded his thinking with incredible sex and contradictory behavior. He needed distance and objectivity to decipher her actions.

"No problem. I will raid the kitchen later. Where is Angeline?"

"Shopping in Marseille."

Ah, yes. Exactly why he was here. To remind himself that a mercenary, self-indulgent heart beat at the core of every woman.

Take his mother, for example. Although his father had never spoken a negative word against her, Franco had been curious enough about the woman who had given birth to him to investigate her death. During one of his university vacations he had researched the police reports and the newspaper stories and discovered that his mother had enjoyed her status as a rich, older man's wife. She had often attended weekend house parties without her husband, and there she'd indulged. In booze. In cocaine. And who knew what else? At one such party, a chemical overdose had killed her at age twenty-six.

His father passed him a glass of wine. "So tell me about this young lady."

"She is an American accountant, a friend of Vincent's fiancée, and she claims she counsels troubled teens in her spare time."

"And?"

"I offered her a million euros to be my mistress for a month. She accepted." But she would not accept all his gifts. That did not make sense. Her honesty had to be a ruse. Who would report a million euros windfall to the tax man and forfeit almost half in taxes?

"She is attractive? Desirable?"

An image of Stacy rising like Venus from the churning waters of the spa flashed in his mind. Droplets had streamed down her ivory skin, clung to her puckered nipples and glistened in the dark curls concealing her sex. Before he had removed the first condom he had been ready to reach for a second. He'd had to dunk beneath the cooling waterfall to regain control. "That was our agreement."

"And yet you're here and she's…where?"

"Monaco. Vincent is pampering his bride-to-be and

her attendants with an all-expenses-paid month at Hôtel Reynard while they plan the wedding. Stacy is a bridesmaid."

"Ah, yes. Vincent is another one making his papa wait for grandbabies. Has he recovered from the accident?"

Vincent had come home with Franco several times during school vacations. Franco had also visited the Reynard home in Boca Raton, Florida. It had been Vincent who had suggested Franco relocate to Monaco for the tax advantages the principality could offer Midas Chocolates. "He is completely mobile now, and through surgeries and physical therapy, has regained 80 percent use of his right hand."

"And his fiancée does not mind the scars or the handicap?"

"She was his nurse in the burn unit. She has seen him look worse." And she had stood by him. Probably because Reynard Hotels was a multi-billion dollar corporation with ninety luxury hotels spread across the globe.

"I look forward to seeing him again and to meeting his bride. I also want to meet your…Stacy, you said? You'll bring her here."

The idea repulsed him. "I do not see the need."

"I do. And is she the kind of woman you would be willing to marry if she refused the money?"

Franco cursed the wording of his agreement with his father, but it would not become an issue. "It will not happen. She has already accepted."

"You seem very certain of that."

"I am."

"When is the money to be paid?"

"The day after Vincent's wedding."

His father turned away, but not before Franco caught a glimpse of a smile. "Just remember our agreement, son."

"How could I forget?"

How indeed? When he returned to Monaco, he would show Stacy the benefits of being a rich man's plaything. Before long she would greedily beg for his gifts instead of refusing them.

And then she would take the money and run.

Alone in Franco's house.

Stacy stood in the foyer after the housekeeper left. Uncertain. Uncomfortable. Undecided. She could be a polite guest and wait in the living room as directed or she could search for signs of obsession. Being a snoop wasn't honorable, but after what she'd learned about her father… She shuddered.

Knowledge was power and she needed all the knowledge she could get about Franco Constantine. Her safety depended on it.

She turned down the hall toward the master-bedroom wing. A twinge of guilt made her pause on the threshold, but she took a deep breath and marched in. The furniture surfaces were clear of clutter. No photographs or knickknacks gave a clue to the room's owner other than big, bold wooden furniture and luxurious linens. The classic landscapes on the wall also revealed little. She would not stoop to pawing through his drawers.

The view of Larvotto through the open drapes lured her, but she ignored it and cautiously opened a door to reveal a closet as large as her apartment bedroom. It looked like a *GQ* man's dream with clothing and shoes neatly aligned on the racks and shelves. There was no sign of a woman anywhere…except for the dress Stacy had left behind the other night hanging alone on an otherwise empty rod with the shoebox beneath it.

She closed the door, returned to the foyer and looked

out the window, but there was no sign of Franco's car. The opposite hallway beckoned. Just past the stairs to the basement she found an open door and looked inside. Franco's study. A large dark-wooden desk dominated the space and tall bookshelves lined the walls on either side of the double French doors opening onto the back patio.

A pair of photographs on one shelf drew her across the room. She lifted one of Franco and another man about the same age standing in front of a picturesque castle. Vincent Reynard. Stacy recognized him from the picture Candace had shown her, but the photo had been taken before the accident that had marred half of Vincent's face. Franco looked at least a decade younger than the man she knew, and his smile was genuine and devastatingly handsome instead of twisted and cynical. Fewer lines fanned from his eyes and none bracketed his chiseled lips. Had this been taken during their grad-school days? But the setting looked European instead of American.

Stacy returned the frame to the shelf. An older man stared out at her from the second photograph. His heavily lined face couldn't conceal the same classic bone structure and cleft chin as Franco. He had Franco's thick hair and straight brows, but his were snowy white instead of coffee-bean dark, and his eyes weren't nearly as guarded as Franco's. Was this Franco's father? She'd never know. And she was okay with that. Really.

Turning slowly, she scanned the tables, sofa and bar cart, but she found no sign of Franco's ex-wife. She returned to the entrance hall and eyed the staircase. Did she dare? What if Franco came home while she was upstairs? How would she explain her snooping without revealing that she'd visited her father's house after her mother's death and what she'd discovered had given her the willies? Franco didn't need to know her tragic past or that her father most likely had been mentally unbalanced. No one needed to know. It was hard enough to make friends without people wondering if she carried her father's defective genes.

Her futile search supported Franco's claim that he was over his wife and his marriage and that he'd moved here after the divorce…unless there was something upstairs. Not that Stacy really cared about his wife, but she wanted to make sure Franco wasn't the type to use his money and power in dangerous ways.

It's not as if you're the kind of woman a man can't forget, especially a man like Franco who must have far more glamorous women than you at his beck and call all the time.

That again raised the question of why he had chosen her?

The sound of a car in the drive made her heart stutter. She hustled to the window, looked out as Franco's black sedan rolled to a stop. Her mouth dried and something resembling anticipation shot through her.

How could she be eager to see him? He was using her. *And you're using him, so don't get sanctimonious.*

He climbed from the vehicle. His gaze searched the front of the house and found her in the window. For a moment he paused with one arm braced on the top of the car and just stared at her. A lump rose in her throat and her heart beat like a hummingbird's wings. He bent and reached inside. When he emerged again and started toward the villa he carried a small white bag with pink ribbon handles that looked too feminine in his big hand.

Another gift she'd have to refuse?

And why did she keep refusing? The diamond bracelet alone could be pawned to pay off her car. But they'd agreed on a price for a service and to keep tacking on extras seemed unethical…. As if there could be anything more unethical than their current agreement. The irony of her situation didn't escape her. But she had to be able to live with herself after this affair ended, and that meant setting standards and sticking to them. It wasn't easy. There had been precious few gifts in her past. And she'd lost the most important one.

She rubbed her bare wrist and then wiped her palms over her pencil-slim skirt and opened the front door. If they were truly lovers this was the point where she'd rush down the walkway to embrace him and welcome him home. Instead, as he approached she stood frozen inside the door unsure exactly what he expected of her.

The closer he came the more shallow her breathing became. While her gaze fed on his lean dark-suited form, he inventoried her lavender blouse, navy skirt and sensible low-heeled pumps. Suddenly she felt dowdy, and she wished she'd slipped into the flirty and feminine sundress hanging in his closet. That she'd even consider dressing to please him rattled her. "Hi."

"*Bonsoir*, Stacy." His arm encircled her waist. He snatched her close, taking her mouth in a ravenous kiss that bent her backward. She clutched his lapels and held tight. Their thighs spliced and the heat of his arousal nudged her belly. His tongue stroked hers and hunger suffused her with embarrassing swiftness.

By the time he released her she was breathless and dizzy, with her pulse galloping out of control. She unfurled her fingers from his suit coat and sagged against the door frame. He swept past her, set the gift bag on the credenza and continued through the living room and toward the kitchen.

Stacy stared at the bag, her curiosity piqued. Maybe

it wasn't for her. After taking a few moments to gather her composure—and to battle the urge to peek into the bag—she closed the front door on the balmy evening and followed him.

Franco had removed his suit coat and laid it over the end of the center island. He held a martini shaker in his hands. The flexing and shifting of his muscles beneath his white shirt as he mixed the sloshing liquid filled her mind with images of those bare muscles bunching and contracting beneath his supple skin as he braced himself above her. She plucked at her suddenly sticking blouse and exhaled slowly.

He poured the contents into a glass and set it on the counter in front of her. Her eyebrows rose.

"You are surprised I noticed you never drink more than one glass of wine at dinner and you ordered fruity drinks at the club?" he asked as he opened a bottle of red wine with practiced ease.

"I guess I am."

He filled his wineglass and lifted it in a silent toast then nodded toward the martini. "Try it."

Stacy lifted the glass and sipped. Chocolate, cherry and vanilla mingled on her tongue. "Very good."

"It is made with Midas Chocolate liqueur." He reached into his inside coat pocket and withdrew a handful of gilt-edged cards which he placed on the counter. "*Le Bal de L'Eté* is this Saturday. I have tickets."

There were more than two tickets in the pile. "A summer ball?"

"*Oui*, it is an annual charity event to mark the opening of the summer season at the Monte Carlo Sporting Club. Europe's *l'aristocratie*, including royalty, attend. You and your friends might even meet the prince."

She gaped. "Of Monaco?"

"*Oui.*"

She'd heard it wasn't uncommon to see members of the royal family on the street or at sporting events, but to meet them... "Will either of the two long dresses you've seen me wear work?"

He shook his head. "*Non.* I will arrange for you—"

"Then I can't possibly go."

"—and your friends to have appropriate gowns," he continued as if she hadn't interrupted.

She sighed. He had her cornered and he knew it. "And if I refuse then Candace, Madeline and Amelia will miss the ball."

He shrugged. "*Tout a un prix.*"

Everything has a price. Yes, he did seem to live by that rule. But how could she deny the other women this opportunity to rub elbows with royalty? "You fight dirty."

"I play to win."

"Okay. On behalf of my friends, I accept." Jeez. That had sounded ungracious. But she hated being manipulated.

"*Bien.* And while you are in an accepting mood..." He left the kitchen and returned moments later carrying the bag. "For you." He held up a hand to stop her protest. "Open it before you refuse."

She reluctantly accepted the bag, withdrew a small box, opened it and gasped. *Her watch.* Hugging it to her chest, she ducked her head, blinked her stinging eyes and struggled to contain the happy sob building in her chest. He couldn't possibly know how much this meant to her. "Thank you."

"You are welcome. The limo driver found it. The band was broken. I had it replaced with a similar one."

"My mother gave me this when I graduated high

school. It was the last gift she gave me before she—"
Her throat thickened, choking off her words.

Franco smoothed his hand from her brow to her nape.
His fingers clenched in her hair and then stroked forward
to lift her chin. "I am glad we found it. Now finish your
drink and then go downstairs and remove your clothing.
The masseuse will be here in ten minutes."

"Masseuse?" Stacy wasn't wild about the idea of
someone else seeing or touching her naked body. She
hadn't joined her suitemates in the hotel spa for sea-salt
massages for that very reason. But she wouldn't mind
Franco's hands on her. "You're not going to, um...
massage me?"

A slow naughty smile curved his lips. "I am going to
watch. And after she has turned your muscles to butter and
departed, I am going to take you on the massage table."

The image he painted sent a shiver of arousal over
her. Stacy realized she was beginning to like not only
Franco, but this mistress stuff too.

And that was definitely not good news.

My God. He had almost hugged her.

Franco fisted his hands and watched the lights of
Stacy's taxi disappear into the night. What kind of fool
was he to be swayed by eyes brimming with tears and
gratitude? And yet when Stacy had looked at him earlier
tonight, clutching that cheap watch to her breast and
smiling through tear-filled eyes, he'd almost succumbed
to the urge to embrace her.

He did not hug or cuddle or any of those other relationship things that would lead a woman to expect more
from him than he could give. And he did not trust tears.
Tears were nothing more than a weapon in a woman's
arsenal. How often had Lisette used tears to get her way

during their marriage? After the abortion she'd tried to soften him by crying and claiming that he'd been spending more time at work than with her, and she'd been afraid he no longer loved her and would not wish to have a baby with her.

Regret crushed his chest in a vise. He *had* spent more time at work during that final year of his marriage. His father's latest divorce settlement had forced him to borrow against the estate, and that meant finding new sources of revenue to cover the debt. Franco had not explained that to Lisette which meant if he were to believe her story, he would have to accept part of the blame for the loss of his child. And that was a burden he could not bear.

Much better to remember that Lisette, like his mother, had been selfish. She'd made a decision she had no right to make without his input, and then she'd tried to place the blame on a scapegoat—him. And of course, there had been more to her story, as he'd discovered the day the hospital released her and his replacement had arrived to carry her to her new home.

He slammed the front door. Stacy Reeves was no different from any other woman. He simply hadn't figured out her strategy yet. But he would. In the meantime, he would make use of her beautiful body and then send her back to her hotel each night until he had his fill of her. And he would sleep alone—as he always did.

"Ohmigod, is that Prince William?" Amelia asked in a hushed voice on Saturday night.

Stacy followed Amelia's wide-eyed gaze over the glittering guests gathered in La Salle Des Etoiles in the Monte Carlo Sporting Club to the tall blond with an aristocratic nose. Stacy had never been a royal watcher. She probably wouldn't recognize a prince if he walked up and shook her hand, but that didn't dilute the excitement of being in the room with the kind of people who graced the pages of the magazines in her former employer's waiting room.

"It could be. Franco said there would be royalty here." In the minutes since they'd climbed from the limo and made their way inside Stacy had spotted at least a dozen American movie stars, two rock idols and a late-night talk-show host. She was so far out of her element it wasn't even funny.

"You want to tell me how you scored tickets for *Le Bal de L'Eté?*" asked Candace, looking stunning in a platinum satin dress. Vincent hadn't been able to get away from the job site to join them, but Candace had handled her disappointment well. "Vincent said they're almost impossible to get unless you're famous or one of the super-rich upper class."

Stacy glanced at her suitemates, each wearing an evening gown Franco had purchased. He'd given Stacy the name of an elite shop on Avenue des Beaux Arts and told her the proprietress would take care of them. "You'll have to ask Franco."

Amelia fidgeted beside her in pale-yellow tulle. "So is it getting serious between you two? Because from where I stand he's looking a lot like Prince Charming and the Fairy Godfather rolled into one very attractive package."

Stacy stroked her hand over the delicate floral beading on her turquoise dress and searched for an answer that wouldn't shock her friends. Telling them the driver had picked her up Monday, Tuesday and Wednesday evenings and delivered her to Franco's villa for sex and dinner probably wasn't the best response. Just thinking about those nights made her tingle.

But Franco had been out of town since Thursday

morning, and her body, which had happily gone without sex for so many years, was having withdrawals. *And withdrawal is all it is,* she assured herself. Just because he'd shown her facets of her sexuality that she'd never known existed didn't mean she was developing an emotional attachment to him. She hadn't missed him or anything mushy like that. Besides, his absence had allowed her to spend time with her suitemates.

She was actually beginning to feel like one of the group instead of an outsider. The bonds of friendship were forming, and tonight while they'd fussed over each other's clothes, hair and makeup in preparation for the ball she'd had a hint of what it might have been like to have sisters. But she wasn't comfortable enough yet to tell her suitemates the unvarnished truth. "Not serious, no. I'm just having a holiday romance as Madeline suggested."

"Are you sure it's not more than that?" Candace asked. "You certainly jumped on that gown the moment the shop owner told you Franco had suggested she help you choose something the color of your eyes."

Heat rushed to Stacy's cheeks. So she wanted to look attractive for him. What was wrong with that? She was beginning to realize he wasn't an arrogant ass even though he did a good imitation of one quite often by pulling away immediately after making love—having sex. But if he were truly a jerk he never would have had her watch repaired or treated her friends to this Cinderella evening. He'd shown his generosity in a dozen other ways outside of bed, like the museum and theater tickets that had been delivered to their suite Thursday morning, the basket of chocolates yesterday and the flowers today. He was showering her with gifts her friends could share—gifts she couldn't refuse without depriving her suitemates.

She shrugged. "He's paying for my gown. He ought to have some say about it."

"Uh-huh," Madeline said, her disbelief clear. She'd chosen a drop-dead-sexy black dress guaranteed to make heads turn, but Madeline seemed to be searching for someone in particular and was unaware of the attention her dress garnered. "Don't get your heart involved, Stace. Remember, we go home in two weeks."

Stacy nodded. How could she forget that in a matter of days she'd either leave Franco and the most sensual period of her life behind or discover she'd repeated her mother's mistake? The first filled her with regret, the second with stomach-twisting apprehension. She forced a smile. "Don't worry about me."

She scanned the crowd searching for Franco. He was supposed to meet them here tonight, but they were a little late arriving. Her gaze collided with his across the room and her stomach took a nose-dive to her sandals. He turned and spoke to the group he was with and then headed in her direction. Her pulse skipped erratically and her mouth dried.

He looked amazing in a tuxedo. Rich. Powerful. Sexier than any man in the room. And hers. For now. The thought filled her with pride...and doubts. Why her when, judging by the heads turning in his wake, he could have any of these more sophisticated women?

Desire flared in his eyes as he climbed the shallow stairs. His gaze lingered on her déeolletage before gliding to her toes and back to her face, and then he took her hand in his and bent to brush his lips over her knuckles. He straightened and looked into her eyes. *"Tu es magnifique, mon gardénia."*

Before she could find her voice he turned toward her companions and bowed slightly without releasing her hand. "*Bonsoir,* mesdemoiselles. *Vous êtes très belle ce soir.* As before, the limo is at your disposal. You will forgive me if I steal Stacy for a dance."

He didn't wait for a reply, but tucked her hand in his arm and led her away. Stacy glanced over her shoulder at the women who offered her a trio of grins and thumbs-up.

On the dance floor Franco pulled her into his arms, leaving her with the sensation of being swept off her feet and into another world—a world in which she wasn't a lonely, staid and unemployed accountant. For a few moments she could pretend to be one of the beautiful, glamorous people who attended exclusive balls, traveled by limousine, rubbed elbows with royalty and captivated a millionaire.

But this wasn't real. She had to remember that.

She laced her fingers at Franco's nape, relishing his slight shudder when she inadvertently teased the sensitive skin with her nails. Each night he'd taught her something new about giving pleasure as well as receiving it. She loved knowing she had the power to make him tremble with desire, but the downside of learning her strength was that her fear of letting anyone get too close faded more with each intimate encounter. Keeping her walls strong wasn't as easy as before—especially when his touch made her feel so alive.

The muscular length of his thighs and torso brushed hers as he swayed to the music. He nuzzled her temple and inhaled deeply, his chest rising to tease her breasts through the thin fabric of her gown. *"J'ai manqué ton parfum."*

She tilted her head back and studied him through her lashes. His passion-darkened eyes cut short any attempt at translating his words. Her skin prickled with awareness and desire smoldered within her. Only inches separated their mouths and the urge to rise on her toes and kiss him tugged at her, but this was his turf, not hers. She didn't know the rules here and until now had never been tempted to make a public display.

"What did you say?"

His lips thinned, as if he regretted speaking. Finally he said, "I have missed your scent."

Her heart stalled and her breath caught. "Me too—yours."

A muscle in his jaw bunched. His fingers flexed against her hips, urging her closer to his thickening arousal. A corresponding heat pooled low in her abdomen. "We must stay until Vincent arrives and then we go. I want you naked and hungry for me."

She gasped and jerked in surprise, but Franco held her close. "Vincent's coming? I should tell Candace. She'll be thrilled."

"It is a surprise. He should be here any moment." He tucked her head beneath his chin. "I must go to Avignon tomorrow. You will accompany me."

She wanted to see where Franco had grown up, but at the same time, her duty to Candace came first. "I don't know if I can, Franco."

"I have paperwork I must peruse. It cannot wait and neither can I." He smoothed a hand over her bottom. The song ended, but he made no effort to release her or leave the dance floor.

Stacy's pulse drummed in the silence. She glanced to where she'd left her suitemates, but they weren't there. "I'll have to check with Candace."

"I have already discussed it with Vincent. He has not seen his fiancée for a month, and he assures me he will not let her leave his bed for the next few days." A flame burned in his eyes. He tightened his arms and melded his hips to hers as the orchestra began another song. "I understand his needs."

She swallowed the lump rising in her throat. Franco wanted her and he made no attempt to hide his desire. What would it be like to have that forever?

Stop it. This isn't about forever—especially not with a man like him.

She tried to pull back, mentally, physically, but the steel band of Franco's arms held her captive. His hands and body subtly rubbed and nudged hers. The rich and famous faces around her blurred as she focused on the man who seduced her at every turn. Moisture gathered in her mouth and much lower. Dancing with him was like foreplay. Her arousal grew so intense she was tempted to find a coat closet and drag him inside. Her face burned and she buried her nose against his neck. How had he turned her from a sexually reticent woman into one who craved his touch so badly she was considering public indecency?

What seemed like eons later Franco said, "Vincent is here. Come."

She glanced toward the entrance and saw a handsome man with brown hair. He resembled the man in the photos she'd seen, and yet Franco led her in the opposite direction. That wasn't Vincent? But then the man in question turned his head to scan the room and Stacy saw the tight, burned skin on the right side of his face. Definitely Vincent. She caught her breath in sympathy. She couldn't imagine the pain he'd endured. Candace had told her about the series of surgeries he'd already undergone and those yet to come.

Franco shot her a hard look and his grip on her hand tightened. "His scars repel you?"

"Of course not. Besides, I knew what to expect.

Candace showed me a picture. She's very protective of him." And from the hard and cool tone of Franco's voice and the warning glint in his eyes, it seemed as if he might be as well. Loyalty to his friends was yet another interesting facet of Franco's personality, but reading him was like trying to decipher a foreign language. There were bits she couldn't understand. "Where are we going?"

"To retrieve his fiancée." They reached a group of women gathered on the far side of the room. "*Excusez-moi, mesdemoiselles.* I must borrow Candace."

Candace frowned. "Is something wrong?"

"*Non.* There is someone you need to see."

Candace noted Stacy's hand held tightly in Franco's and a smile curved her lips. "Having a good night?"

Stacy's face and neck warmed. "Yes."

"And it is about to get better," Franco muttered for Stacy's ears only, sending a flash fire through her.

He led them toward the entrance and stopped at the bottom of the stairs where Vincent waited with love in his eyes so intense Stacy's heart stuttered.

Candace spotted him, squealed and launched herself into his arms. Given Stacy's already erotic thoughts, witnessing their passionate kiss made her squirm and glance at Franco. His thumb stroked over the inside of her wrist and his eyes promised *soon.* Her pulse tripped.

The couple drew apart, hugged and parted again with blinding smiles. And then Vincent turned to Franco. The men embraced and exchanged a few words too quiet for Stacy to overhear in the noisy ballroom. The genuine affection between them surprised Stacy. To date, Franco had seemed somewhat aloof except when in seduction mode.

When they parted, Candace dragged Stacy forward. "Stacy, this is Vincent. Vincent, Stacy."

Vincent extended his hand. Ignoring the scars, Stacy shook it. From Candace she knew he'd come a long way in his recovery, but other people's squeamishness sometimes bothered him. "It's good to meet you, Stacy."

"You too, Vincent. And thank you for this once-in-a-lifetime vacation."

"You're welcome. Anything that keeps Candace from overdoing it with the wedding plans works for me." Vincent encircled Candace's waist and spread his left hand possessively over her still flat belly. The couple exchanged another intimate, love-laden glance.

What would it be like to have a man look at her that way?

The rogue thought staggered Stacy. Suddenly it hit her that she would never experience the bond that Candace and Vincent shared. Until now that hadn't concerned her. In fact, being alone and safe was a path she'd deliberately chosen, but now the solitary life she'd planned yawned ahead like a barren stretch of desert road.

Because of her bargain with Franco she'd soon have a home. But it would be empty.

She'd never fall in love.

Never experience the hope, joy and anticipation of having a child with someone she loved—all of the emotions written clearly on Candace's face.

Stacy would live alone. Die alone. And the world would be no different because of her time in it.

Sadness settled over her like a cold, wet blanket. Every lesson she'd learned to this point had made her afraid to let anyone get too close. But she'd found the courage to make friends. Could she also find the courage to allow a man into her life and into her heart?

Not a powerbroker like Franco. But maybe someone tamer. Someone less wealthy. Someone she could trust. If such a man even existed.

Eight

Stacy had shared intimacies with Franco that made her blush, and yet she still knew very little about him beyond the physical. She hoped a night in his family home would fill in a few of the blanks.

"Do you always buy your women?" she asked to fill the silence during the hours-long Sunday-afternoon car ride to Avignon.

Franco's jaw hardened and he shot her a chilly glance. "I have never offered a woman money for sex before you."

If that was supposed to make her feel special, it failed. "Good, because it seems a little like…prostitution."

"It is supply and demand. You have something I want and I am willing to pay your price. Relationships always come at a price, Stacy. If you do not believe that then you are deceiving yourself. I prefer to have the terms stated up front rather than be unpleasantly surprised in the end."

Would anyone willingly enter a relationship if they knew the costs going in? Stacy's fling with the high-school jock had cost her her self-respect, and her short-lived involvement with a coworker had diminished her confidence. But her mother had paid the ultimate price for loving the wrong man.

Stacy pushed the memories away and studied Franco's profile, the way he brushed his thick dark hair away from his brow, his straight nose, his sensuous lips and square chin. Beard stubble already shadowed the line of his jaw even though it was barely two in the afternoon. "As an accountant I often see the effects of costly divorce settlements. Is that what happened in your case?"

Seconds passed as Franco exited off the autoroute and onto a narrower road. She wondered if he'd avoid answering personal questions the way he usually did. She'd given up on getting an answer when he said, "Money was not the issue. My wife had an abortion. I did not know she was pregnant or that she did not want children."

No wonder he was bitter. "I'm sorry. Did you want a large family?"

"It was assumed I would provide heirs."

"You still could."

"I will not marry again."

She felt a quick stab of…something. Regret? Of course not. It didn't matter to her if Franco didn't want another wife. What he did once she left Monaco was none of her business. And she wanted it that way.

A few minutes later he turned down a long, straight tree-lined driveway. When they reached the clearing at the end of the drive Stacy mouthed a silent, "Wow."

The white stone structure with its round twin towers flanking opposite corners looked like something from a fairy tale. Flags bearing coats of arms fluttered from the conical spires. It looked familiar and then she placed it as the building in the background of the picture of Franco and Vincent in Franco's study.

"You grew up in a castle?"

"*Un château.* There is no moat, drawbridge or curtain wall."

Castle, chateau, whatever. "No wonder you were able to get tickets to the ball. You're one of them. The aristocracy."

A twinge of envy stirred inside her—not for his wealth, but for the childhood he must have had. "You and your siblings must have loved playing here."

"I am an only child."

"Me too." As a child she'd longed for someone to play with, and as a teen she'd just wanted to belong somewhere and to have someone to confide in. Always being the new kid and an outsider had been difficult.

The cobblestone courtyard circled a round multi-tiered fountain. Wanting to absorb every detail, she barely waited for the car to come to a stop before she shoved open the door and leaped out. Moments later Franco joined her beside the gurgling water. "How long has the chateau been in your family?"

He shrugged. "A few hundred years."

"A few hundred *years?*" Stunned, she faced him. "Do you have any idea how lucky you are?"

"How so?"

Regretting her revealing outburst Stacy bit her lip and stared at the parapets and then panned the acres of emerald lawn. "You've always had a home to go to. A place where you belonged."

"You did not?" he asked quietly.

"No." She turned toward the trunk. "Let's get the luggage. I can't wait to see the inside of the chateau."

He caught her arm in a firm, but not painful grip. "Explain."

She didn't want his pity, but if her past could keep him from taking this spectacular place for granted then what would it hurt to tell him? "My mother left my father when I was eight. After that we never lived in any one city for more than a year."

"They divorced?"

"No. He refused to grant her a divorce, so she ran away."

"Why did she run?" He drew mind-numbingly erotic circles on the inside of her bicep with his thumb.

"According to the diaries I found after she…died, my father was physically abusive. She wrote that she left the first time he struck me. I don't recall being hit, but I do remember my mother sending me to my room whenever my father started yelling. And I remember the fights and arguing and the sound of my mother crying. I remember kissing her boo-boos." The last phrase came out in a strangled whisper as the past descended over her like a dark, oppressive cloud.

He muttered something she suspected was a curse. "Why did she not have him arrested?"

Feeling chilled despite the sunny day and warm temperature, Stacy pulled away and hugged herself. "She tried once, but my father was wealthy and powerful. He had friends in high places and the hospital records of her injuries mysteriously disappeared, so the charges were dropped. In her diary she claims reporting him only made him angry and vindictive."

"You said earlier that your mother had to choose between food and rent. Could she not demand monetary support from your father?"

"No. She wrote that the one time she called for help he threatened to kill her if he ever found her." The memories rose up to choke her and a shudder slithered through her. She'd never confessed the full extent of her past to anyone. She didn't know why she wanted to now except perhaps she wanted Franco to understand why financial security was so important to her. For some reason it was important that he know greed hadn't been the motivating factor in accepting his proposition. "One day he did."

A moment of shocked silence stretched between them. "*Mon dieu*. What happened?"

"I came home from my first class in night school and found my mother and a man I didn't recognize dead in our apartment. The police identified him as my father. He'd found us with the help of a private investigator. The CSI guy said my father shot my mother and then himself."

She squeezed her eyes tight against the memory of red blood pooled on the white kitchen floor and having to walk through it to see if her mother was still alive, and then rib-crushing panic when she realized she wasn't.

Franco yanked Stacy into his arms and hugged her tight enough to squeeze the breath from her lungs. One big hand rubbed briskly up and down her spine. His lips brushed her forehead. She leaned into him, absorbing his strength and accepting comfort in a way she'd never allowed herself before, but then she gathered herself and withdrew, because leaning on him was a habit she couldn't afford. But she instantly missed his embrace.

The empathy in his eyes made hers sting with unshed tears. "So now you know why I accepted your proposition. I want a home. Nothing as grand as this. But a place that's all mine."

"What of your father's estate? If he had wealth, then why did you not inherit?"

A question she'd asked herself countless times

until she'd learned the truth. "He left everything to his alma mater."

"And you did not contest his will or file a wrongful death suit?"

She shifted on her feet and studied the sunlight reflecting off the windows of the chateau. "No. Either would have cost money I didn't have. And I couldn't risk running up years of legal fees and then losing and being in debt."

"Stacy, no court in the States would have denied your right to his estate after what he took from you, and a lawyer would have accepted you as a client with payment contingent upon a settlement."

She dug the toe of her sandal into the gravel drive and debated full disclosure. What did she have to lose? She lifted her gaze to Franco's. "Immediately afterward, I wondered if I could have stopped him if I'd been at home, and I said as much to the police detective. He told me that from the extra bullets in the gun and the photographs of me in my father's rental car, they suspected he had intended to kill me too."

The ultimate betrayal. A parent who wanted her dead.

"By starting school and changing my schedule I wasn't where he thought I'd be." She walked to the back of the car, struggled to regain her emotional footing and waited for Franco to open the trunk.

"After that I didn't want anything from him except answers which he couldn't give me. The executor of the estate let me walk through my father's house before the auction. Mom's makeup table looked like she'd gone out for the day and would return any minute, and all the clothing she'd left behind hung in the closet even though she'd left eleven years before. My room was the same. It was like a shrine to an eight-year-old girl. It creeped me out."

"And you had no one to turn to?"

"No one I trusted." *Trust.* There was that word again. She realized she was beginning to trust Franco and that couldn't be good. He was rich. She hadn't seen signs of him abusing his power or the law, but she'd known him less than two weeks.

"You have accomplished much by moving on instead of letting your past destroy you." The approval in his voice wrapped her in a cocoon of warmth.

"I didn't want my mother's sacrifice to be in vain. She left to protect me."

He stroked his knuckles along her cheekbone. "You have done her proud."

His words were a soothing balm she hadn't known she needed, and the tenderness in his eyes made her yearn for something, but what exactly, she wasn't sure. She stepped closer.

"Franco, Franco, Franco," a childish yell splintered the intimate spell. Stacy flinched and backed away. Close call. She couldn't afford to become dependent on him or his approval.

Franco lowered his hand and turned to the small boy bolting from the chateau. The child raced down the walk and launched himself at Franco who caught him, swung him in the air and then hugged him while the boy talked far too fast for Stacy to translate the words. Franco replied in the same language, his voice low and tender.

Stacy couldn't help but stare. Franco looked relaxed and happy. A wide smile transformed his handsome face into a knee-meltingly gorgeous one. If he ever looked at her that way she'd completely forget about his wealth and all the other reasons why he was the wrong man for her.

Who was the boy? Franco had said he and his wife

hadn't had children and yet the affection between the two was unmistakable. She guessed the child to be about six or seven.

Franco set the child on the ground and ruffled his dark hair. "Stacy, this is Mathé. Mathé, this is Mademoiselle Reeves. Speak English for her, please."

Mathé's small left hand clutched Franco's larger one as he shyly mumbled a hello and quickly shook Stacy's hand. Big brown eyes peeked at her before turning back to Franco with idolization shining in their depths. "Are you staying?"

"*Oui,* for the night. Go tell your *grandmère* we will need two rooms." The boy rushed off.

Stacy's gaze followed him back to the house. "He's cute."

"The housekeeper's grandson. He has lived here with her since his mama ran off with her lover and left him behind three years ago." The bitterness in his voice raised a number of questions.

"He's about the same age your child would have been."

Doors slammed in Franco's expression. Any remnants of his smile vanished. He extracted their suitcases and slammed the trunk. "Do not try to paint me as a hero or a sentimental fool. I am neither."

"Whatever you say. But he's clearly thrilled to see you."

"I spend time with him when I can. He has no father and mine is too old to keep up with him."

"*Entrez-vous?*" An older man called from the open front door. Stacy recognized him from the photo in Franco's study.

"*Oui,* Papa. We are coming." Franco carried the luggage toward the house. Stacy followed. "I have come to look over the documents you had drafted."

"You are staying the night?" Stacy thought he asked.

"Oui."

Her French had improved tremendously in the past two weeks, but Stacy quickly lost track of the heated rapid-fire conversation that followed. Whatever his father said turned Franco's face dark with anger.

Franco turned to her. "It appears my soon-to-be stepmother has decided to redecorate the house. All of the bedrooms except for mine and Papa's have been stripped."

"We could go to a hotel," she suggested.

"Not necessary. Stacy, is it? I am Armand Constantine. Welcome. Come in." He extended his hand. "It is not as if you and Franco are not already sharing a bed. I am old, but I am not old-fashioned or easily shocked."

Embarrassment sent a scalding wash across her skin. "It's nice to meet you, Monsieur Constantine."

She shook his hand and followed him inside. The detailed plasters, gilt-framed artwork and period furniture in the entrance hall screamed history—a history Stacy had never had as her father's house had been built after Stacy's birth. A wide staircase worthy of a romantic Hollywood movie soared upward from the center of the grand hall.

"Franco, show Stacy upstairs and then bring her to the salon for refreshments."

Franco remained motionless for several seconds and then nodded stiffly and climbed the stairs. Stacy followed, her eyes drinking in the original oils on the walls, the beautiful antiques and the endless halls. Finally, Franco shoved open a door and walked into a round room that looked as if it belonged to a teenage boy.

She quickly averted her gaze from the double bed covered in a blue spread. Her pulse skipped erratically at the thought of sharing the narrow mattress with him.

Sleeping with him—something she had yet to do. "Your bedroom's in a tower."

"Oui." The clipped word drew her gaze from the boyish decor to his face.

"I guess your stepmother didn't get to your room yet?"

"My room is off-limits to her as it has been to each of my father's four wives." He dumped their bags on a large wooden trunk beneath one of the five windows punctuating the walls.

"He's been married four times?"

"Five if you count my mother. He likes to fall in love. Unfortunately, he falls out of it rather quickly. But not before each of my stepmothers has her turn at emptying the bank accounts and erasing all traces of the previous Madame Constantine from the chateau."

No wonder he thought every woman had a price. She'd learned more about Franco in the past half hour than she had in the previous two weeks. She'd thought the chateau meant Franco had enjoyed the stability and permanence she'd lacked, but apparently not if he had revolving stepmothers and his home was always being torn apart.

Shelves loaded with sports memorabilia lined the walls. The trophies and ribbons drew her to the side of the room. Bicycle racing. Swimming. Rowing. That explained those wide shoulders and muscular legs. She'd never lived anywhere long enough to join a team, and at one time she'd condemned her mother for that. Stacy had lost count of the times during the past decade she'd wished her bitter words back.

She dragged her fingers along the spines of a series of books on car racing. Franco's cologne teased her nose a second before the heat of him spooned her back and his hands settled at her waist. She leaned into him.

"I took Vincent to the Monte Carlo Grand Prix after our grad-school graduation twelve years ago. He became hooked on fast cars. When he returned to the States he convinced his father to sponsor a NASCAR team."

And last year he'd been badly injured at a race.

Stacy turned. Franco stood so close their hips and thighs meshed and she could see the tiny strain lines radiating from his eyes and lips. "You can't blame yourself for his accident. Candace said it was a freak event. Something about an equipment failure."

He hesitated. "There is a price for each choice we make."

"*Tout a un prix,*" she quoted his earlier words back to him. Everything had a price. Including her.

Would the price for this affair end up being more than she could bear?

Franco needed to get away from Stacy. *Now.*

He had broken a rule and hugged her. How could he not? She might have tried to act unaffected while telling her grisly tale, but the tremor in her voice and the deathly pallor of her face had given her inner angst away. If she was acting, she was the best damned actress he had ever seen.

But if she was telling the truth then not only had her mother walked away from money, but Stacy had as well. She could not possibly be that different from other avaricious members of her sex. Could she? Had she not already hinted that a million dollars would not be enough to give her a life of leisure?

But she plans to go back to work. She did not ask for more.

What was it about her that made him talk? He had revealed things about Lisette and Vincent that he had never shared with anyone. If he did not leave now then there was no telling what she would extract from him.

He put necessary inches between them. "I must read over the documents and spend an hour with Mathé. Can you amuse yourself?"

"Of course," Stacy replied without hesitation.

"If you are genuinely interested in history then you may explore the house. The wives are allowed to change the linens, but not the furniture or the architecture."

Excitement flared in Stacy's eyes. Any of his other lovers would have pouted if he tried to ignore them, and then they would have cajoled or attempted to seduce him into entertaining them. If he had brought his lovers here, that is. And since Lisette, he had not. Stacy would not be here if not for his father's insistence on meeting her. Franco would not put it past the old goat to have stripped the rooms himself to force Franco to share his bedroom and his bed.

"Your father won't mind if I snoop around?"

"*Non.* Papa knows the history of the house and the furnishings. I will see if he can accompany you."

"I don't want to be any trouble." She fussed with a button on her blouse and Franco struggled with a sudden urge to strip the garment from her. He had escorted her from his bed to a taxi less than twelve hours ago, and yet his desire for her had not diminished with exposure. If anything, his craving for her had intensified. Not a positive circumstance. "Your father wasn't expecting me, was he?"

"He asked to meet you."

Her eyes widened. "You told him about me? About us?"

"*Oui.*"

"The whole truth?"

"I do not lie." Her gaze fell and her cheeks darkened.

From embarrassment? Was she ashamed of the bargain they had made? Franco reached out and tucked a stray lock of hair beneath Stacy's ear. "Tonight, we will do something I have never done."

Her pulse quickened beneath his fingertips. "What's that?"

"I have never had a woman in my boyhood bed. Fantasies, *oui*. But flesh? *Non*."

Her gaze darted to the object in question behind him and the tip of her tongue dampened her lips. He could not resist bending down to capture and suckle the soft, pink flesh. Stacy leaned into him, curling her fingers around his belt and rising on her toes. Her breasts pressed his chest with tantalizing softness.

She had come a long way as a lover. In a short time she had become less reticent about her pleasure, but she had yet to initiate any contact. He was on the verge of saying to hell with the documents and tumbling her onto the sheets when she pulled away. Blushing, she ducked her head as if her ardent response embarrassed her. "Go. I'll be fine."

He didn't want to leave her, and for that very reason he escorted her to the salon where his father waited with refreshments, then walked out and locked himself in his father's study.

The documents transferring ownership of the Constantine holdings to Franco, less a lifetime annuity for his father, were straightforward. His father had agreed to sign the papers the day Stacy returned to the States with her million. Franco delayed as long as he possibly could, rereading the document and then playing with Mathé before going in search of Stacy two hours later.

He found her in the nursery, sitting in an old rocking

chair with her head tipped back and her eyes closed. Her slender fingers caressed the worn wooden arms.

His mood lightened at the sight of her. And what nonsense was that? Why did Stacy affect him so strongly? Was it because she did not try to work her wiles on him? Or did she have him completely fooled? Was her air of innocence the bait in her trap?

"Que fais-tu?" he asked, more harshly than he had intended.

She startled and her lids flew open. "I'm imagining what it would be like to rock your baby in the same chair that your mother and grandmother used. It must be comforting to know that generations of ancestors have sat here and had the same hopes and fears for their children. Any child would be fortunate to have roots that deep, Franco."

An image of Stacy rocking with a dark-haired baby at her breast—his baby—filled his mind. He rejected the possibility. No matter how logical her motivations, he'd bought her, and he could not respect a woman he could buy. "I doubt my mother ever rocked me in that chair. She was not the loving type. I had a series of *bonnes d'enfants.*"

"Nannies?"

He nodded.

"My mother was wonderful. We moved a lot and she worked most of the hours in the day, but I always knew she loved me." Stacy rose, hugged herself and walked to the window. The curtains had been removed, leaving the wide casement bare to the evening sun. "She was my best friend even though I wasn't always the best of daughters. I hated moving, and once I hit my teens we argued about it often. But that's because I didn't know why. She always told me my father loved me and wanted to be with me, but that he couldn't."

"She lied."

She abruptly faced him with her head held high, her hands fisted by her side and fire in her eyes. "To protect me, yes."

"My father lied as well, but during a school vacation I researched the newspaper archives and learned the truth about my mama. She was a spoiled party girl always looking for excitement. Shopping. Drugs. Men."

The sympathy softening Stacy's eyes made him regret the confession. Confidences would lead her to expect more from him than he was willing to give. He was a cold bastard—or so he'd been told. Stacy would do best to accept his limitations and his money and move on.

"I'm sorry. I assumed living in a wonderful place like this meant you'd automatically have a happy childhood."

"I was not unhappy." And why was he sharing that? Because he did not want her pity.

"Are you and your father close?"

"When he is not enthralled with his latest paramour, *oui*. We used to go to the races together." She was getting too personal. He had to derail this tête-à-tête.

Franco approached her, pinning her in the window by planting a hand on either side of her. He leaned closer, inhaling her unique scent and aligning his hips with hers. Desire thickened his blood. "I have not made love in this room either and we have an hour before dinner."

That he considered sex less personal than conversation was telling, he realized. The understanding he saw in Stacy's eyes took him aback. She saw through his actions, but rather than call him on his evasive tactics, she smiled and cupped his cheek. "I'm all yours."

For two more weeks. Longer would be too dangerous. Stacy had a way of breaching his defenses. He would have to find a way to stop her before he crumbled like castle ruins at her feet.

Nine

Franco's laughter stirred something deep inside Stacy.

She crossed from the luxurious en suite bathroom to one of the tall tower windows of Franco's bedroom and looked outside. Franco and Mathé were kicking a soccer ball around on the lawn below. Franco's teeth flashed in the early-morning light as he laughed again.

He'd be a good father. The kind of father she wished she'd had. And his children would have all the things she'd lacked. History. Roots. Security.

According to Monsieur Constantine, this room hadn't changed in over two decades. Franco could have had something new with each of his stepmothers' redecorations, but instead he'd stuck with the furnishings he and his father had chosen together. That told Stacy Franco liked stability. And he might even have a tiny sentimental streak. Like her.

She touched a finger to her watch and then smoothed

a hand over the scarred wooden headboard pushed against the wall between two windows. Last night she'd slept spooned with Franco on the narrow mattress. This morning she'd awoken alone, but surprisingly well-rested. Letting her guard down enough to sleep had apparently not been an issue after all. But then again, he had exhausted her before letting her sleep. Warmth rose under her skin and settled in her pelvis. The man seemed determined to make up to her for the mediocre lovers of her past.

"You are exactly what Franco needs, my dear," Monsieur Constantine said in heavily accented English behind her.

Startled, Stacy turned and found him in the open bedroom doorway. Hadn't Franco said he'd told his father the whole truth? "How can you believe that?"

The older man shrugged. "I am sure you had your reasons for agreeing to accept money in exchange for spending time with my son. But you are not like any…how you say?…gold diggers I have ever encountered. I have met many in my seventy-five years, and I have even had the misfortune to marry a few. Between my wives and Lisette, my son has become quite bitter and distrustful of women."

Stacy nodded. "He told me about Lisette."

Bushy white eyebrows rose. "That is surprising. Did he also tell you that he continued to love her until she admitted she had married him for his money, and that she had the abortion because she was planning to divorce him?"

Poor Franco. "Um…no."

"My divorce settlements put us in financial difficulties. Difficulties over which Franco eventually triumphed, but his wife did not have the integrity to lessen her expenses and stand beside him through adversity. When one truly loves one takes the good with the bad…as I did with Franco's mama."

He joined her by the window and looked down on Franco and Mathé. "He will not tell me what Lisette said to him in that Paris hospital, but it changed him. He is not the son I once knew. He keeps much locked inside now."

The weight of his gaze settled on Stacy. "My boy has a wounded soul. It will take a special woman to heal him."

What exactly was he implying? "Why are you telling me this, Monsieur Constantine? I'm not that woman."

"I believe you are."

A choked sound of disbelief erupted from her mouth. "I'm sleeping with your son for money."

"And the agreement troubles you, yes?"

"Of course."

"And that is but one of the reasons I know you are not like the others."

Keeping up with the bizarre discussion was beyond her. He might as well be speaking a foreign language. "One of the reasons?"

"*Oui.* If you cared only for financial gain you would be garbed in jewels and designer clothing instead of your inexpensive American pieces. Franco is a generous lover. Except in matters of the heart."

True. But his loyalty to Vincent and Mathé came from the heart, so he wasn't incapable of caring. "Dare I ask if there are more reasons?"

The older man smiled. "Only the most important one. When I gave you the tour of the chateau yesterday you asked many, many questions about the history of the house and furnishings. You never once asked the value of a single item."

No, she hadn't. She'd been more concerned with the

sentimental significance than the monetary worth. "I guess I never thought about the costs."

"*Exactement.* For a woman who claims to be motivated by money, it seems to have little importance to you."

Other than the security it represented, he was right. She didn't want to be rich. She just wanted a home. Otherwise, she would have sued her father's estate as Franco had suggested. Heaven knows the lawyers had aggressively solicited her and encouraged her to do so before she'd fled Tampa and started over in Charlotte. But she hadn't wanted to be tied to blood money. She'd rather be poor than feel guilty for profiting from her mother's murder. "Okay, you have me there, but I'm still not the right woman for Franco."

"We shall see, Stacy. I am hoping my son will see what a treasure you are before it is too late." He offered his arm in the same courtly gesture Franco often used. "Now come, breakfast waits and you should eat before you make the drive back to Monaco."

"And once every inch of your ivory skin is slick with the sun-warmed tanning oil I will thrust deep into your body again and again until you cry out as *le petit mort* overcomes you," Franco resumed his tantalizing tale after they crossed Monaco's border and turned toward the harbor.

Stacy's heart raced. She licked her dry lips and squirmed in her seat, attempting to alleviate the ache between her legs.

Franco had filled the past half-hour of their trip with a lengthy, detailed description of the sensual afternoon he had planned for them on his sailboat. His verbal seduction was a timely reminder that their relationship was all about sex. Only sex. Any emotional connection she might feel with him after the personal insights she'd gained into his character at the chateau had no place in the bargain they'd struck.

His fingertips trailed up the inside of her thigh. "And I will not stop until—"

An annoying sound interrupted him and dampened her arousal. A cell phone. Hers. Stacy blinked, exhaled and dug her phone out of her purse. "Hello?"

"Candace is having a meltdown," Amelia's voice said. "Madeline and I have tried everything we know to calm her down. It's your turn."

"What do you mean?"

"She's freaking out and talking about cancelling the wedding. We can't figure out why. You have to try. Tell her how much money she'd be wasting or something. Not that money would matter if she was really unhappy, but she's absolutely crazy in love with Vincent. We can't let a flash of panic ruin that. Please, Stacy, just get over here convince her to sit tight until rational thought returns."

Alarmed, Stacy glanced at Franco. "I can be there in fifteen minutes."

She disconnected and turned in her seat. "I'll have to take a rain check on the boat ride. That was Amelia. She wants me at the hotel."

"Something is wrong?"

"Um…Candace needs me." Because he was Vincent's friend she couldn't tell him why. But she wanted to. She wanted to ask him how someone as deeply in love as Candace could have doubts.

"And what of our plans?"

Stacy had never been on a boat, but that wasn't the appeal. She wanted to spend more time with Franco, wanted to learn more about him. She'd planned to ask

questions during the car ride home, but his verbal seduction had waylaid that. Had he done it deliberately?

"Franco, I would love to spend the afternoon with
you. And making love on the boat sounds amazingly
sexy even though I'm not sure about doing it outdoors
on the deck where we might be seen by anybody with
a good set of binoculars. But when Candace needs me
I have to go, and you promised our relationship
wouldn't interfere with the wedding stuff."

His jaw hardened. "Vincent assured me your
presence would not be required for several days."

She should have tried harder to check with Candace
before leaving for Avignon, but the bride-to-be hadn't
been in the hotel suite Sunday morning or answering her
cell phone. In the end, Stacy had let her curiosity about
Franco lead the way. "Vincent was wrong."

Franco turned the car away from the marina and
toward the hotel. Moments later he stopped the vehicle
outside the entrance. A doorman opened her door and
helped her alight. She thanked him and joined Franco
by the trunk.

She reached for her bag, but Franco held it out of
reach. "I will see you inside."

Not a good idea since she had no idea what she'd be
walking into. "No need. I'll…um, call you later."

He looked ready to argue, but instead he relinquished
her suitcase and stroked her cheek. The passion simmering in his intensely blue eyes snarled a tight knot of
desire beneath Stacy's navel. "Dinner tonight. I will
send the car."

"I'll have to clear it with Candace first."

He nodded. "I will let you go, but first—"

Heedless of the hotel staff members and vacationers
around them, he took her mouth. Hard. Hot. Intimately.

His tongue delved, stroked and then he suckled hers. By the time he lifted his head Stacy clung dizzily to his belt. "Do not keep me waiting one moment longer than necessary, *mon gardénia*."

He stroked a thumb over her damp bottom lip and then left her standing in the driveway on trembling legs, torn between desire and friendship. She wanted to go with Franco, but Candace needed her.

Stacy shook off her indecision. Her friendship with Candace would continue beyond the next two weeks, but her relationship with Franco would not. And she'd better not forget it. Passion and profit were all she could expect from him. No promises, he'd said. And that wouldn't change no matter how well she understood him.

She marched inside and across the lobby. The elevator whisked her to the top floor. Stacy shoved her keycard into the lock and entered the suite in time to hear Candace ranting, "I can't believe he expected me to drop everything and spend three days in his bed."

Amelia spotted Stacy, grabbed her by the arm and dragged her into the sitting area. "Good. You're here. Tell her how crazy it would be to cancel the wedding at this late date."

Stacy let her purse and overnight bag slide to the floor. "What's wrong?"

Candace pivoted. A white line of tension circled her compressed lips. "I can't marry Vincent."

Stacy blinked. "Why?"

"Why does everybody keep asking me that?" Candace glared at them and then paced in front of the long window. "Can't you just accept I made a mistake and leave it at that?"

"No," Amelia and Madeline chorused.

"Don't you love him?" Stacy persisted.

"I wouldn't be here if I didn't."

And the love in Vincent's eyes at the ball had been impossible to miss. "Did something happen to make you no longer trust him? Did he scare you? Threaten you? Hurt you?"

"No." She sounded surprised Stacy would even suggest it, but then she didn't know Stacy's past. One day, Stacy realized, she'd have to tell her. But not today.

"Then I don't understand why you'd throw this all away. Do his scars suddenly repulse you?"

Anger flushed Candace's pale cheeks. "No. They. Do. Not."

"Then why can't you marry him? You love him and he clearly adores you."

"It's like you said. He's rich and powerful and I'm…not. I don't fit into his world. The balls, the limos, the designer gowns, they're not me."

"They're not any of us, but we've had fun faking it," Amelia said.

Stacy recalled Monsieur Constantine's words about Franco's ex. "Candace, would you still want to be with Vincent if he lost all his money?"

"Of course I would. I don't know what you're getting at, Stacy, but I am not marrying Vincent for his millions. I thought you knew me better than that."

"My point is, doesn't he deserve a woman who'll love him for who he is as a person and not for the penthouse lifestyle he represents? And doesn't the fact that you don't care about the scars or the superficial trappings and that you could live without the limos and designer clothes make you the perfect woman for him?"

And didn't Franco deserve the same thing? His father was right. It would take a special woman to appreciate the man beneath the glitz. Someone who didn't assign dollar signs to everything or mind slowly chipping away at his hard shell to discover his secrets.

Someone like you.

Stacy gasped in surprise as the thought sprouted and took root. It would be so easy to convince herself she was the woman who could heal Franco's embittered soul. But that would be foolish. Besides, he wouldn't be interested in a nobody like her when he had a continent full of glamorous, sophisticated women to choose from. And she…well, she couldn't risk it.

"Yes. No. I don't know." Candace sank onto the sofa and buried her face in her trembling hands.

Madeline sat beside her and passed her a tissue. "You have been happier this year than I've ever seen you. Do you really want to throw that away because of bridal jitters?"

"What I want doesn't matter." Candace blotted her tear-stained face. "Vincent's parents are arriving tonight. He wants to tell them about the baby, and once they find out they're going to think I trapped their precious son with a pregnancy to get my claws on their fortune."

Tension seeped from Stacy's muscles upon hearing the true reason for the panic attack. This was a salvageable situation. She glanced at her suitemates, but neither Amelia nor Madeline looked surprised about the baby news. Hmm. Maybe the baby wasn't a secret after all.

Stacy sat on Candace's opposite side and tentatively laid a hand over her clenched fist. "You're afraid to tell your future in-laws you're pregnant?"

"They're Boca Raton and I'm trailer trash. They're not going to want somebody like me raising their grandchild."

Stacy understood the feeling of not fitting in all too well, but running had never made it better. "Number one, Candace, you're not trailer trash. You're a registered nurse. Number two, I suspect the Reynards are going to want someone raising their grandchild whose love will stay strong through the good times and the bad."

"That would be you," Amelia said.

Stacy nodded. "Don't forget what you've already been through with Vincent. I'm sure they haven't."

After a moment Candace's lips curved into a quivery smile. She looked at each of them in turn and then took a shoulder-straightening breath and lifted her chin. "You're right. I am the perfect woman for Vincent, and if the Reynards don't agree, well…I'll just prove them wrong."

"We've got your back," Madeline vowed.

Stacy wished she had half as much confidence as her friend in matters of the heart. But she didn't. She was an emotional coward and probably always would be.

"Don't ever fall in love, man," Vincent groaned into his beer.

"That is not what you have been telling me for the past six months," Franco replied as he sat on the opposite end of the sofa from Vincent and pressed the remote control to his plasma television. He tuned his satellite dish into an American sports channel. "You have been singing the praises of a woman to warm your bed."

Vincent wore a besotted expression similar to the one Franco had seen on his father far too often—one Franco swore never to wear again. Lisette had cured him.

"It's more than regular sex. It's waking up beside her and watching her sleep. Or knowing she loves you enough to let you see her without her makeup on or to kiss her before she brushes her teeth."

The back of Franco's neck prickled. He shifted his shoulders to ease the uncomfortable sensation. He had watched Stacy sleep this morning at the chateau, but that had nothing to do with love. It had been lust. Nothing more. And the kiss on her brow had been an attempt to wake her and satisfy his hunger. If in the end he had elected to take a cold shower and let her sleep, it was only because he had driven her to orgasm so many times last night that he doubted her capable of coming again so soon, and he never left a woman unsatisfied in bed.

"Fifty bucks says the Marlins whip Boston," Vincent said, drawing Franco's attention back to the baseball game. "Women aren't logical. And they're full of contradictions."

"I agree, and I accept your bet." He had finally found Stacy's weakness. She could be bought but only if the gifts benefitted her friends. Such altruism had to be a pretense.

"Women are like a jigsaw puzzle with missing pieces. Frustrating. Unsolvable. And I ought to know. I must have put a hundred puzzles together during my hospital stay."

"You will get no argument from me." Each secret he uncovered about Stacy suggested she was not like the other women of his acquaintance, which only meant he needed a more complete picture to uncover her strategy. He glanced at his watch. When would she call?

Vincent had phoned immediately after Franco had left Stacy at the hotel ninety minutes ago. Watching baseball with his friend was not the sexually satisfying afternoon Franco had planned, but he could not concentrate on work, and he had been a Red Sox fan since his days at MIT.

Vincent's expression turned to one of bewilderment. "When I told you I'd keep Candace busy I honestly thought she and I would spend every spare minute of the next three days making up for four weeks' abstinence. But this morning I mentioned my parents were flying in today and that I wanted to tell them about the baby, and she freaked."

"Due to your parents' arrival or to revealing the pregnancy?"

"Don't know. That's the illogical part. Candace and my parents get along, and in another month or two she'll be showing. No point in trying to hide it. Besides, I don't want to. I spent years avoiding getting a girl pregnant, but the minute I found out Candace was carrying my baby I wanted the world to know. Candace is the one who insisted we keep a lid on it. Besides, my folks will be thrilled to finally have a grandkid on the way since my sister isn't anteing up."

Franco's father was impatient as well. Impatient enough to force Franco's hand. Franco's mind flashed back to the image of Stacy in the nursery rocking chair, her wistful expression before she'd known he was watching and the sadness in her eyes when she'd talked about her mother.

Stacy's life had been tragically difficult, but it had not broken her. He had to respect her strength even though he disliked her willingness to sell herself for financial security. How hypocritical of him, since he benefited from her mercenary streak.

Vincent swore as a Sox batter hit a grand slam. "If they keep this up I'll owe you for more than the tickets to the ball and that killer dress you bought for Candace."

"There is no need to repay me."

"Bull. You and Toby are babysitting these women at my request. I'll cover all the costs, and I'll grant you a year's lease on a Midas Chocolates location in the galleria of the Aruba hotel." He popped a handful of nuts in his mouth and washed them down with a sip of beer.

"The hell of it is, Franco, that when I was stuck in

labor negotiations, Candace is all I thought about. And I got pissed—not because the union rep was being a prick, but because he was keeping me away from Candace. It's hard to care about dollars and cents when I'm scared as hell that I'm going to blow it with her. She's the best thing that's ever happened to me, and if having my lady-killer mug back meant never having met her, I'd rather keep the face that frightens children."

Surprised by the emotional speech from a man previously not given to sentiment, Franco drained his beer. Stacy had invaded his concentration at work as well this past two weeks. No woman had ever done so—not even Lisette. The only positive in the situation was that his preoccupation would end as soon as she boarded the plane bound for the States. "The scars are less noticeable with each surgery and graft."

"Yeah, but unlike you, I won't win any beauty contests."

The doorbell rang, wiping the smile from Franco's lips. He was not expecting anyone. Normally, he would be at work on a Monday afternoon. *Stacy?* No, she would call and his cell phone had not rung. He had checked twice to make sure it was turned on. "Excuse me."

He crossed the entrance hall and opened the door. Stacy stood on the porch looking as delicious as a juicy peach. A wide-brimmed straw hat covered her chestnut hair and a pale-orange sundress outlined her curves. Her bare legs looked magnificent despite the bulky walking sandals she insisted on wearing.

The breath stalled in his lungs, but his heart raced. He caught a glimpse of a taxi's taillights turning out of the drive.

A tentative smile wobbled on her lips. She removed her sunglasses, revealing her azure eyes. "Is it too late to go boating?"

"Vincent is here." He found her fading smile and obvious disappointment surprisingly gratifying since it mirrored his own. He used his thumb to free her bottom lip from her teeth. "Come in."

"I don't want to intrude. I'll just call a cab." She reached for her cell phone, but he caught her hand.

"*Non.* Stay." He dragged his knuckles along her arm. She shivered, reminding him of last night, of tasting every inch of her delectable skin until she whimpered and squirmed. "You may sunbathe by the pool. I will drench your body in suntan oil, and when the game ends I will send Vincent in search of Candace and we will have the sybaritic afternoon we anticipated, but on dry land. My patio is private. No one will see or hear when I make you cry out in ecstasy."

Her breath hitched and her nipples pushed against her dress. "Okay."

He motioned for her to precede him. Stacy crossed the foyer and entered the den. Franco noted that she avoided stepping on the rugs. He filed the odd fact away for later.

Snapping his cell phone closed, Vincent rose. "Hi, Stacy. Rain check on the game, Franco. Candace called. I have to go."

Vincent shook his head when Franco smirked. "You're laughing now, but one of these days a woman will have you dancing to her tune."

"That will not happen, *mon ami.*"

"Just wait, bud. Your day will come. I'll see myself out." A moment later the front door closed behind Vincent. The engine of his Ferrari roared and then faded in the distance.

Franco turned to Stacy. "Remove your clothing."

She gasped and clutched her bag tighter. "Here? Now?"

"*Oui.*" He tugged his shirt over his head and pitched

it onto the sofa. He retrieved the condom from his wallet before dropping his trousers and briefs and kicking off his shoes and removing his socks. Stacy watched wide-eyed and then licked her lips as she stared at his growing erection. The slow glide of her tongue over her rosy flesh made him pulse with need.

She turned her back. Franco swept her silky hair aside, unzipped her dress, flicked open her bra and shoved both to the floor. He dragged her panties down to her ankles, pulled her back to his front and cupped her breasts. For several seconds he fought the urgency to be inside her and simply savored the feel of her warm, soft skin against his and the weight of her breasts in his palms. He inhaled her scent and his control wavered. He stepped away. "Come."

He led her outside, dropped the condom on the table and then arranged the double-width lounger to his liking. He took the straw tote which she held in front of her like a shield and set it on the tiles. Despite Stacy's apparent shyness, her nipples were erect and desire flushed her face and neck.

"Lie face down."

She crawled onto the chaise, presenting him with her delectable bottom. He fisted his hands against his rampant hunger.

"You have suntan oil?" His voice came out an octave lower than usual.

"I have lotion in my bag."

"*Pas le même chose.* Not the same. I will return momentarily, and then, *mon gardénia,* I will make you moan."

An all-over tan had never been one of Stacy's goals. She didn't even have the courage to try on one of the thong bikinis so prevalent on the beaches here. And forget going topless.

She could not believe she was naked on Franco's patio. Glancing left and right, she verified that this spot was indeed private, thanks to the vine-covered trellises at each end of the house. The sun warmed parts of her it had never seen before. And then Franco returned, striding boldly, *nudely,* in her direction. He had a pair of towels tucked under his arm, a bottle of suntan oil in one hand and one of water in the other.

Her heart pounded faster. She dampened her dry lips. If anyone had ever told her a month ago that she could become a hedonistic creature she'd have called them delusional.

"Close your eyes," he said as he dropped the items he carried beside her on the chaise and straddled her legs. Stacy did so, admitting she'd probably brought this on herself by telling him his masseuse had not turned her on. What Franco had done after the masseuse left, on the other hand…. The memory sent a delicious tingle through her. Suffice to say she would never view the long wooden benches of a sauna in the same way again. If she ever saw the inside of another sauna.

Warm oil trickled over her shoulders and back, quickly followed by Franco's firm hands. The scent of coconuts filled her nostrils as he massaged her with long, slow strokes across her shoulders and down her spine. His fingertips teased the sides of her breasts, her waist. The occasional drag of his sex against her buttocks made her breath catch. He paused, shifted and then oil dribbled onto the small of her back and over her bottom. It seeped into the crevice and between her legs to her most sensitive spot. She squirmed on the chaise.

Franco's hands stilled her hips. *"Non."*

He alternated feather-light brushes with muscle-deep massages over her back, her bottom, down her legs and across the soles of her feet. Throughout the process the wiry hairs on his legs teased her hyper-sensitive skin. And then he stroked his erection between her slickened cheeks. Stacy yearned to rise to her knees and let him take her from behind as he had once before, but he moved away. The memory of that night in front of his bedroom mirror, the way he'd cupped her breasts and nibbled her neck, the undiluted hunger on his face as he'd plunged into her again and again made her shiver.

"*Attente elle,*" he ordered in a gravelly voice.

Wait for it. One of his favorite phrases. But Stacy didn't want to wait. She wiggled impatiently, but Franco didn't quicken his torturous caresses. Arousal pulsed through her. She no longer cared about prying eyes, but focused instead on the man who seemed bent on driving her out of her mind with desire. He rose from the chaise and she tensed in anticipation.

"Turn over."

Stacy hastily complied. Franco's shaft glistened with suntan oil. She reached for him, but he shook his head and pulled the brim of her hat over her face. "No peeking."

She settled back into the cushion. Oil trickled over her breasts and slowly ran down her sides like tiny, warm fingers. He poured another pool in her navel and then drizzled more over her curls. His palms covered her breasts and she gasped. He teased and tweaked, rolling the slick tips between his fingers and buffing with the flats of his palms. She shifted her legs, but that only intensified the ache. His massage continued down her torso and her legs, skipping her neediest parts.

Stacy was ready to beg when Franco bent her knees, knelt between them and stroked his shaft along her soft, slick folds and against her center. A moan slipped from her lips as she rose swiftly toward the peak. She heard a snick of sound, and then icy-cold water splashed her nipple. She squealed and tried to rise, but Franco planted a palm on her breastbone and treated the opposite side to the same cold, fizzy bath. The carbonated water teased in an unbelievably sensual way, and then his hot lips covered a cooled tip. He alternated between icy baths and hot suckling until Stacy batted her hat away.

"That was sneaky."

He sat back on his haunches, his grin unrepentant. Two could play that game. She sat up, snatched the water from his hand and drenched his erection. His howl turned into a groan when she took him into her mouth.

Franco fisted his hands in her hair, but he didn't thrust or try to gag her the way her high-school lover had. Franco let her take the lead and as much of him as she could handle. Pleased and surprisingly turned on, she released him and showered him with another splash of water and then another deep kiss. His back arched. He hissed with each splash and muttered what sounded like encouragement in French each time her lips encircled him. She smiled and repeated the process until the bottle was empty.

She had never expected to like doing this, but the tendons straining Franco's neck and his knotted muscles attested to his enjoyment. And she liked pleasing him.

"Tu es une sirène." He tugged gently on her hair, but firmly enough to make her release him.

A siren? Her? She smiled.

He reached for the condom he'd tossed on the table earlier, tore the wrapper with his teeth and then sheathed himself. Stacy reclined and opened her arms. Franco guided himself to her center and plunged deep. The sun-warmed latex over his hot shaft added yet another new dimension to his erotic play. She savored the sense of fullness, rightness, and then tangled her legs around his waist the way he'd taught her and held on tight. He took her on a roller-coaster-fast ride to the top and then she plunged over to the sound of him calling her name as he climaxed.

Their gasps filled a silence broken only by the hum of the pool filter and an occasional bird call. Stacy stroked a hand down his sweat-dampened back. "Wow."

He levered himself up on his elbows. "You have hidden talents, *mon gardénia.*"

A blush warmed her cheeks. How could she still blush around this man? "I've had an excellent teacher."

"And there is yet much to learn," he said gently as he pulled away. And then he stilled and stiffened. *"Le condom, c'est cassé."*

Stacy's heart missed a beat. Her muscles turned rigid. She prayed she'd mistranslated. "What?"

Franco's serious gaze locked onto hers. "The condom broke."

A wave of panic seized her. Her gaze dropped to the damning evidence, and her heart nearly beat its way out of her chest.

Dear God, was she going to repeat her mother's mistake?

Calendars, dates and biology scrambled in her head, and then sanity slowly invaded, making sense of it all, but leaving her cold, drained and eerily calm. She exhaled shakily. "My…um, period is due in a few days. We should be safe. I'm…um…unlikely to conceive now."

"How regular are you?" he asked without blinking.

She flinched, and feeling exposed, dragged a towel over her nakedness. Would she ever get used to these intimate conversations? "Like clockwork."

"Bien. But to be certain you will visit my doctor

before you return to the States. I will make the appointment." As if that settled everything, he straightened, crossed to the pool and dove in.

But Stacy was far from settled. She pressed a hand to her chest. Close call. Too close. She wasn't prepared to have a baby or let a man into her life.

Or was she?

Ten

A baby.

And not just any baby. *Franco's baby.*

The words reverberated in Stacy's head as the taxi carried her back to the hotel. Guilt nagged her for sneaking out while Franco was in the shower, but she couldn't calmly sit across the dinner table from him or go back to bed with him until she figured out the chaotic emotions churning inside her.

Her chances of getting pregnant today were slim. And that was good news. Wasn't it?

Absolutely.

This was the wrong time, the wrong place and the wrong man.

But there was a tiny spark of something that felt suspiciously like hope glowing deep inside her. Illogical, foolish hope. The idea of having a baby appealed, even though she hadn't once thought about having children since learning the truth about her mother's murder.

Had being around Candace activated some twisted kind of approaching-thirty biological clock?

She pressed a hand to her agitated stomach. Franco had the means to buy and sell her a hundred times over, and after his painful experience with Lisette there was no telling how he'd react if Stacy turned up pregnant.

Would he want the child or tell her to get rid of it?

"Mademoiselle, we have arrived," the taxi driver's words jerked Stacy back to the present before she could pursue that disturbing line of thought. She blinked and saw the hotel entrance outside the car window. The ride had passed in a blur.

A uniformed hotel employee opened her door. She dug the appropriate money from her wallet, paid and tipped the driver and climbed from the cab.

Standing on the pavement, she debated going up to the suite. But Madeline was far too perceptive. She'd zero in on Stacy's disquiet in seconds, and as much as Stacy longed for a dose of the savvier woman's no-nonsense advice or the support she knew her trio of suitemates would offer, she needed to get her thoughts in order first.

Stacy stepped onto the sidewalk and headed toward Monaco-Ville with no particular destination in mind. She loved the old-world charm, the sense of history and permanence in the oldest part of the principality. That it happened to be in the opposite direction to Larvotto Beach and Franco's view was an added bonus.

For the past ten years she'd focused on her safety and her financial security, but she'd completely neglected the emotional component of her life. She'd been afraid to let anyone get close and had paid for it with loneliness. Not even the teens she counseled were allowed past her emotional barriers. She cared about them, but knowing they might pack up and move without notice led her to maintain a protective distance.

But she didn't want to be alone or afraid anymore. She liked having friends, liked feeling connected and wouldn't mind having a family.

If she were pregnant, she wouldn't get rid of the baby no matter what Franco said. With his million euros she could afford to keep it, and even without his money she could manage once she found another job.

But could she deny a father his child or a child its father, live life on the run, always looking over her shoulder and never set down roots or make a home? No. She wouldn't wish her childhood on anyone. Not unless she truly feared for her own or her child's safety.

She didn't see Franco as being that kind of threat.

Didn't your mother's diary and your father's actions teach you anything? Rich men can't be trusted.

But she'd seen no sign of Franco being power-crazed or bending the laws to suit his needs. Other than buying her, that is. But as he'd pointed out, mistresses were not unusual here, and he'd shown her nothing but respect. He'd made sure that each sexual encounter left her satisfied when he didn't have to. He'd watched over the bridal party for Vincent, and he took the time to play with a fatherless boy—almost every weekend, according to Monsieur Constantine.

From everything she'd seen, Franco was a good man, and she suspected he'd be a good father.

Oh my God. Are you falling for him?

The leaden feeling in the pit of her stomach said yes.

Her steps slowed and her internal warning sirens screamed.

Had she learned enough about her own strength and resilience over the past decade to lower her walls and let a man in? Maybe. The training she'd had before and since she'd begun volunteering with the teens had taught her what constituted a healthy relationship. Surely she could practice what she preached?

A child's laughter startled her. Stacy looked around, stunned at where her subconscious had led her. The Saint Martin Garden was one of several playgrounds Monaco had set aside for children. She'd walked past it the day she'd toured the Prince's Palace. Sinking down on a bench in the shade, she studied the happy faces of the mothers and children.

Monaco would be a wonderful place to raise a family. According to her stack of guide books, the schools were good and the police force was second to none. Education and safety had been her guideposts in recent years.

Whether or not today's encounter resulted in a baby, would Franco want more than the agreed-upon month? Would he be interested in her staying in Monaco to see if their relationship had a future after the other bridesmaids flew home? She and he were both wounded souls who feared trusting and being hurt. Could she heal him and in the process learn to trust again?

Could he be happy with her? She couldn't compete with the elegant women at the ball, but the remarkable chemistry between them had to account for something, didn't it?

Confidence swelled within her. She could do this. She would face her fears and ask him to give their relationship a try.

Her cell phone rang. Stacy checked the number on the caller ID. Franco's. Her heart raced and her palms dampened. She couldn't talk to him right now. Her decision was too new, too raw, so she silenced her phone.

Tomorrow she'd be ready to take that colossal leap.

A baby.

The idea didn't repulse Franco as much as it should have. In fact, having a child with Stacy could solve many problems. If he provided an heir, his father would not feel the need to impregnate the tramp plotting to empty the Constantine coffers. And Stacy wanted financial security. They could each benefit from continuing their relationship.

He tried Stacy's cellular number again and once more received her voice mail. He disconnected rather than leave a third message. Why had she left without saying goodbye? And why would she not return his calls?

By the time he had finished working out his tension by swimming laps, she'd been in the lower-level shower. He could have joined her, but he had needed a few moments alone to consider the ramifications of their situation. In all his thirty-eight years he had never had a condom break. He had retreated to his bathroom, and when he had exited his shower Stacy had been gone.

Had Candace phoned? Had Stacy's wedding duties once more taken precedence over her agreement with him? Was she having a relaxed dinner with her suitemates at this very moment while he paced his living room?

He looked forward to his evenings with Stacy more than he should, and he would not mind spending more time with her. She was attractive, intelligent and an extraordinary lover. She did not cling or make demands on his time that he was not willing to offer.

She is getting too close. And if you do not quit focusing on her absence you will be no better than your besotted friend.

He turned on the TV, but not even a baseball game tied in the bottom of the ninth inning with bases loaded could hold his attention. His thoughts kept straying to Stacy, her belly growing round with his child. But he could not afford to be deluded by a woman's false promises again.

What if Stacy were pregnant? Would she, like Lisette, choose to abort his child? Could he stop her?

He wiped a hand over his face. No. He would not engage in a legal battle to force a woman to carry a child she did not want. His only options lay in convincing her she wished to continue the pregnancy and in coming to an agreement satisfactory to them both regarding the child.

Stacy could not possibly be as pure-hearted as she pretended. He would prove it. And once he did then perhaps she would quit monopolizing his thoughts.

"I want you to have my baby," Franco said Wednesday night.

Stacy's heart and lungs stalled at the bald statement. She stared into his somber eyes across the secluded table in Le Grill, the ritzy rooftop restaurant at the Hôtel de Paris.

Her heart lurched back into motion and she dragged oxygen into her deprived lungs. Warmth and cautious optimism trickled through her.

Franco must have spent the forty-eight hours since the broken-condom incident thinking about a future together—as she had. She'd barely been able to concentrate on her bridesmaid's duties. She'd lost track of the number of rehearsal-dinner place cards she'd messed up yesterday and how many times the seamstress had asked her to stand still during her final dress fitting today.

"Your baby?" The words filled her with a tingly sensation. He offered her more than she'd ever dared hope for. Financial security. A home. The possibility of a family. A man who would treat her like a princess the way her mother had promised.

"*Oui.*"

"I might not be pregnant."

"A circumstance we can easily rectify."

Was this a proposal? It had to be. Why else would he bring her to this romantic restaurant where the roof retracted to allow the patrons to dine beneath a blanket of stars? But Franco didn't pull out a ring or get down on bended knee. Maybe the French didn't follow that custom? "I've, um…been thinking about that too."

"You would have to leave your job—a job you claim to love."

She clenched her napkin in her hand, looked away from his intense gaze and confessed, "No, I won't. I was laid off the week before we left for Monaco. I didn't tell Candace because I didn't want her worrying about me when she had a wedding to plan."

Franco's jaw hardened. "You are unemployed? You said you would go back to work when you returned to the States."

"I plan to search for a job, but there are a lot of companies downsizing right now. Not knowing how long it would take for me to find another position is another reason I accepted your offer. But now I don't have to worry about that. I wouldn't mind working here until the baby comes. Afterward—"

"I will pay the expenses on your apartment in Charlotte until you return. And of course, you will be compensated."

Confused, she blinked and frowned. "What?"

"I will give you another million euros upon the birth,

and I will cover all the medical expenses you and the baby incur."

Dizziness threatened to topple her. She grasped the edge of the table and studied his face, but she didn't see any trace of emotion or romance. In fact, he looked as if he were closing a business deal. "A-are you asking me to marry you, Franco?"

He reared back in his chair. "*Non.* I need an heir. You want financial security. I am offering a solution to fill both our needs. A second million will give you the life of leisure you claim the first would not."

The delicious shrimp appetizer she'd consumed turned to molten lead in her stomach. Her chest felt so tight she could barely breathe. "You want me to have a baby…and hand it over to you? Gr-grant you sole custody?"

"*Oui.* As you have seen, I can provide many advantages for a child."

The horror of his words chilled her to the bone and pain speared through her like shards of glass. Oh my God. She'd fallen in love with the arrogant bastard.

Impossible. She hadn't known him long enough to fall in love with him. But merely liking him and being disappointed in him wouldn't hurt this much.

"You don't want me? You only want to buy my baby?" For clarity's sake she rephrased her questions. The words burned her throat. She had to be wrong. He couldn't be asking that.

"*Tu es très* sexy, Stacy. I will enjoy sharing your bed for however long it takes to produce a child. But I have no desire for a wife."

He had clearly stated that he would never marry again on their ride to Avignon. Why hadn't she listened? Franco was alone by choice. He would never allow a woman to get close to him. And he would never change.

She might be willing to lower her walls and risk her heart, but he wasn't.

How could she be so stupid? She'd been falling in love with him and he'd been setting her up. She shoved back her chair and stumbled to her feet. "No."

Franco rose. "I will give you twenty-four hours to reconsider."

Déjà vu. "Don't hold your breath. This time I won't change my mind. You can take your two million euros and shove them up your fine French a—"

"*Y a t'il un problème, mademoiselle?*" an anxious waiter asked.

"Yes, there's a problem. I feel ill. I'm leaving." She turned back to Franco. "I don't ever want to see you again."

"Stacy, if you end this now you will forfeit the money."

And she'd be right back where she started. Nearly broke and out of a job. Too bad. There were some things money couldn't buy.

"Your price is too high. I could never have a child and let it go." A chill swept over her when she realized what she'd said and that she meant it to the bottom of her soul. There was more of her father in her than she'd ever realized. She gulped down a wave of nausea. "And I could never respect a man who would ask me to do so."

She gathered her wrap and her purse and raced for the exit before her tears could escape.

"You were right about Angeline."

His father's voice drew Franco from his contemplation of the Fontvieille harbor far below his thirtieth-floor office window. He swiveled his chair to face the door and the desk and the profit and loss statement he had been neglecting. "What happened to her?"

"I told her I was considering transferring ownership

of the Constantine holdings to you and she left." Pain, disappointment and resignation deepened the lines on his father's face.

"I am sorry." But good riddance.

Armand sank down into the leather visitor chair. "She reminded me of your mother. They all do. Young. Vibrant. Beautiful."

"My mother was unfaithful. Why would you want another woman like her?"

"Francesca was always faithful to herself. I made the mistake of believing my love would transform a party girl who needed to be the center of attention into a loving wife and mother. But true love does not require change. And giving her free rein in hopes that she would be happy and always come home to me was not fair to you. I should have put a stop to the drugs the moment I found out about her habit, but I was afraid doing so would drive her away."

Franco digested the surprising insight into his parents' relationship.

"You were right about Stacy," he admitted reluctantly.

He had waited eight days for her to call and tell him she'd changed her mind. Eight days of being unable to concentrate or sleep well. But the only communication he had received from her was a box delivered via courier containing the gifts he had given her—except for the watch band. She had kept the gift he could buy with pocket change.

Where was the greed, the sense of entitlement that his other lovers had had?

His bed was empty. And there was a barrenness to his days and nights that had not been there before. Even Vincent's bachelor party last night had not lightened his mood.

"Stacy refused the money?"

"She walked away from our agreement when I offered her another million to have my baby."

"I assume that was a proposal."

"Non."

"You asked her to bear a child and then relinquish it to you?"

"Oui."

His father shook his head sadly. "For someone who is worried about our liquid assets you are throwing around a lot of money."

An accurate charge. "It was a test."

"To see if she was…what did you say? Ah yes, a duplicitous and mercenary creature who would sell you anything you wanted to buy?"

Franco nodded.

"And she refused."

"She said my price was too high."

"That would explain why our employees have been ducking for cover for the past week." Franco arched an eyebrow and his father shrugged. "I may have retired, but I have my sources."

Armand tapped the file against the sharp crease of his trousers. "So you have finally found a woman you cannot buy. What are you going to do about it?"

Franco fiddled with his pen and remained silent. He did not have an answer. He'd had confirmation this morning from a physician that Stacy was not pregnant. The news did not bring him any relief from the edginess riding his back.

"Our agreement was that you choose a woman you would be willing to marry if she could not be bought. I will not hold you to that because a marriage should never be based on anything but love." His father stood and tossed the file folder onto the desk in front of Franco.

"The documents are signed. You do not have to marry to gain control of the Constantine holdings. It is yours. But perhaps you wish to marry to regain your heart."

Taken aback, Franco stared at his father. "I do not wish to marry again."

Armand planted his fists on Franco's desk and leaned forward. "She is not like Lisette, Franco. This girl cares nothing for your net worth."

No. Stacy was nothing like his selfish ex-wife. But opening himself up for another evisceration held little appeal. "I know, but the risks—"

"Bah. When did you become a coward? Love is a gamble, but when it is true the rewards far outweigh the costs. Being alone and right is a poor substitute for being happy and in love—even if that love is imperfect." He straightened. "What will it cost you to let Stacy get away? Can you live with always wondering who is putting the smile on her face? Who is warming her bed? Think about that, hmm?"

His father turned for the door without waiting for an answer, but paused on the threshold. "I will see you at Vincent's rehearsal-dinner party this evening. Perhaps by then you will have your answers."

After his father left, Franco opened the document folder. The signature on the bottom line made Franco the sole owner of the Constantine holdings, including the chateau and Midas Chocolates. He had more to lose now than ever before.

In two days Stacy would return to the States. A wise man would let her go. Only a besotted fool would beg her forgiveness and ask her to stay.

"He's here," Madeline whispered.

Stacy's stomach clenched into a tight knot, but she kept

her back to the entrance of the private dining room in the upscale Italian restaurant hosting the rehearsal dinner.

She'd known Franco would be here tonight, but that didn't mean she was ready to face him. Only Madeline knew the full truth of Stacy's situation, and that was because she'd caught Stacy in a weak moment, dragged her for another late-night meeting in the bar and pried the sordid story out of her. Stacy didn't want to dampen Candace's happiness so she'd sworn Madeline to secrecy.

"Want me to keep him away from you?"

A smile tugged Stacy's lips at the mother-hen tone of her suitemate's voice. "I don't think that will be necessary. But thanks."

If Franco had missed her or discovered any feelings for her at all, he would have called. But Stacy hadn't heard from him since she'd left him in the restaurant last week. She swallowed to ease the tightening of her throat.

She, on the other hand, kept second-guessing her decision. She loved him more than she'd ever thought she could love anyone, but he obviously expected every woman to leave him as his mother, his father's exes and Lisette had done. If Stacy stayed with him but delayed getting pregnant, could she convince him in time that she wasn't like the other women in his life?

Her gaze shifted to Candace and Vincent's love-struck faces. Franco had never looked at her that way—with his heart and his soul in his eyes. She yearned for him to.

Technically, the bride and groom had been married earlier this evening in a private civil ceremony the way French and Monegasque law required, but they were waiting until after the church service tomorrow morning to actually begin their lives as husband and wife.

"What's he doing here? He's not on the guest list," Madeline said in a panicked whisper.

"Who?" Stacy turned toward the door. Her gaze landed on Franco in a dark, custom-fitted suit and her heart ached. She quickly looked away before meeting his gaze and spotted the man who'd posed as Madeline's tour guide—a man who'd turned out to be anything but the humble tour guide he'd led Madeline to believe he was.

The color completely drained from Madeline's face. She squeezed Stacy's hand. "Stacy, I don't want to abandon you, but I cannot face him right now. Go with me to the ladies' room?"

Stacy squared her shoulders. She would not run. Her running days were over. "No. Go ahead. I'm okay. Franco is seated at the opposite end of the table from me. I can avoid him until after dinner. Longer, if I'm lucky."

If not, she'd survived her mother's murder and her father's betrayal. Facing Franco couldn't be worse than that. Or could it? She felt as if her heart were being ripped out all over again.

Needing a few minutes to bolster her defenses, she slipped out onto the colonnade. In forty-eight hours she would not have this magic view of Monaco, but no matter what happened she would always be grateful for her time here. She'd learned that despite her dysfunctional youth she could fall in love, but she could let go—unlike her father.

"Why do you not tread on my rugs?" Franco asked from behind her.

Stacy winced and wished she'd had a few more minutes to prepare for this encounter. She took a bracing breath and turned to find him a few yards away. He stepped out of the shadows and her lungs emptied again when she noted the lines of stress marring his handsome face. She shook off her concern. If he was stressed, it was no more than he deserved. He'd tried to buy her baby.

"I had to walk through pools of blood on our white kitchen floor when I found my mother and father. Your red rugs on white marble remind me of that night."

"I will throw the rugs out and replace the floor if you will come back to me."

Her heart stuttered. "What?"

He closed the distance between them. "I was wrong, Stacy. All the money in the world cannot buy the one thing I desire most."

"An heir? I'm sure you can find some woman who'll jump at the chance."

His unwavering blue gaze held hers and something in their depths made her pulse skip. "I desire you, *mon gardénia.*"

His velvety deep voice sent a tremor rippling over her. She held up a hand to halt his approach. "Don't do this, Franco."

But he kept coming until her palm pressed his chest. His warmth seeped through his silk shirt into her fingers and snaked up her arm. She jerked her hand away and fisted it by her side.

"I was afraid to trust what my eyes—what my *heart*—told me. I offered to buy your baby as a test. If you had accepted the money, then I would know you were like every other woman I have known. But you are nothing like them."

She couldn't comprehend what he was saying, but that look in his eyes was beginning to fan that ember of hope she thought he'd extinguished. "Why me?"

A smile flickered on his lips. "Besides your incredible legs and the contradiction between the siren in your eyes and your cloak of reserve?"

"Huh?"

"Because my father challenged me to find a woman I could marry if she couldn't be bought."

Had someone slipped something into her drink? "I'm sorry?"

"Papa suggested I stop dating spoiled rich women and find someone with traditional values if I wanted to find a woman who would love me for myself and not my money. I told him I would prove him wrong by finding one of the mythical paragons he described and buying her."

Stacy flinched. She'd thought she couldn't possibly feel worse, but she did. Had she been nothing more than a bet? He lifted a hand to stoke her cheek, but she jerked out of reach. "So taking me to the chateau was just flaunting me in front of your father to show you'd won?"

"*Oui.* That was my original goal. But then you told me about your parents. You had compelling reasons for accepting my offer. Reasons which I could not condemn. And you refused to let me spoil you with meaningless gifts. I found myself falling in love with you." He extended his arms, palms up and shrugged. "I had to push you away."

Falling in love with her? She pressed a hand over her racing heart. "I would have slept with you without the money, Franco."

"And I would have offered you more." He stepped closer and trapped her by planting his hands on the railing beside her. "So much more."

He really had to stop doing that. She told herself to duck out of the way, but her legs seemed numb. He bent and teased the corners of her mouth with tantalizing, but insubstantial and unsatisfying kisses.

"*Je t'aime,*" he whispered against her lips and her world stopped. Taking advantage of her shocked gasp, he captured her mouth in a deeply passionate kiss. And then he slowly drew back, his lips clinging to hers for a heartbeat longer.

The emotion in his eyes washed over her, but she was afraid to believe what she saw.

"I love you, Stacy, and if you can find it in your heart to forgive me, I want to marry you. I will add fidelity to my vows, because I never want you to doubt that my heart and my soul belong only to you. And whether or not we have children, the money I promised you is yours because you have given me so much more than money can buy."

Her eyes burned and her throat clogged. Happiness swelled inside her. Only a man who truly loved her would offer her everything she'd ever dreamed of and at the same time open the door to set her free and provide her the means to escape.

He loved her enough to let her go.

"You don't have to buy my love, Franco. It's freely given."

"Tout a un prix."

A smile wobbled on her lips. She cupped his cheeks and stroked her thumbs over his smooth warm skin. "Not this time. I love you, and if you lost everything today, I would still love you tomorrow and every day thereafter. Yes, Franco, I will marry you."

His chest rose on a deep breath. "I swear you will never regret it, *mon gardénia*."

* * * * *

Don't miss the next book in the
MONTE CARLO AFFAIRS series!
Look for
THE PRINCE'S ULTIMATE DECEPTION
by Emilie Rose
coming July 2007 from Silhouette Desire

THE ROYAL HOUSE OF NIROLI
Always passionate, always proud

The richest royal family in the world—united by
blood and passion, torn apart by deceit and desire

Nestled in the azure blue of the Mediterranean Sea, the
majestic island of Niroli has prospered for centuries.
The Fierezza men have worn the crown with passion
and pride since ancient times. But now, as the king's
health declines, and his two sons have been tragically
killed, the crown is in jeopardy.

The clock is ticking—a new heir must be found
before the king is forced to abdicate. By royal decree
the internationally scattered members of the Fierezza
family are summoned to claim their destiny. But any
person who takes the throne must do so according to
The Rules of the Royal House of Niroli. Soon secrets
and rivalries emerge as the descendents of this ancient
royal line vie for position and power. Only a true
Fierezza can become ruler—a person dedicated to their
country, their people…and their eternal love!

*Each month starting in July 2007,
Harlequin Presents is delighted to bring you
an exciting installment from*
THE ROYAL HOUSE OF NIROLI,
*in which you can follow the epic search
for the true Nirolian king.
Eight heirs, eight romances, eight fantastic stories!*

Here's your chance to enjoy a sneak preview of the
first book delivered to you by royal decree…

FIVE minutes later she was standing immobile in front of the study's window, her original purpose of coming in forgotten, as she stared in shocked horror at the envelope she was holding. Waves of heat followed by icy chill surged through her body. She could hardly see the address now through her blurred vision, but the crest on its left-hand front corner stood out, its *royal* crest, followed by the address: *HRH Prince Marco of Niroli...*

She didn't hear Marco's key in the apartment door, she didn't even hear him calling out her name. Her shock was so great that nothing could penetrate it. It encased her in a kind of bubble, which only concentrated the torment of what she was suffering and branded it on her brain so that it could never be forgotten. It was only finally pierced by the sudden opening of the study door as Marco walked in.

"Welcome home, *Your Highness*. I suppose I ought to curtsy." She waited, praying that he would laugh and tell her that she had got it all wrong, that the envelope she was holding, addressing him as Prince Marco of Niroli, was some silly mistake. But like a tiny candle flame shivering vulnerably in the dark, her hope trembled fearfully. And then the look in Marco's eyes extinguished it as cruelly as a hand placed callously over a dying person's face to stem their last breath.

"Give that to me," he demanded, taking the envelope from her.

"It's too late, Marco," Emily told him brokenly. "I know the truth now…." She dug her teeth in her lower lip to try to force back her own pain.

"You had no right to go through my desk," Marco shot back at her furiously, full of loathing at being caught off-guard and forced into a position in which he was in the wrong, making him determined to find something he could accuse Emily of. "I trusted you…."

Emily could hardly believe what she was hearing. "No, you didn't trust me, Marco, and you didn't trust me because you knew that I couldn't trust you. And you knew that because you're a liar, and liars don't trust people because they know that they themselves cannot be trusted." She not only felt sick, she also felt as though she could hardly breathe. "You are Prince Marco of Niroli…. How could you not tell me who you are and still live with me as intimately as we have lived together?" she demanded brokenly.

"Stop being so ridiculously dramatic," Marco demanded fiercely. "You are making too much of the situation."

"*Too much?*" Emily almost screamed the words at him. "When were you going to tell me, Marco? Perhaps you just planned to walk away without telling me anything? After all, what do my feelings matter to you?"

"Of course they matter." Marco stopped her sharply. "And it was in part to protect them, and you, that I decided not to inform you when my grandfather first announced that he intended to step down from the throne and hand it on to me."

"To protect me?" Emily nearly choked on her fury. "Hand on the throne? No wonder you told me when you first took me to bed that all you wanted was sex. You *knew* that was the only kind of relationship there could ever be between us! You *knew* that one day you would be Niroli's king. No doubt you are expected to marry a princess. Is she picked out for you already, your *royal* bride?"

* * * * *

Look for
THE FUTURE KING'S PREGNANT MISTRESS
by Penny Jordan in July 2007,
from Harlequin Presents,
available wherever books are sold.

Mediterranean NIGHTS™

Experience the glamour and elegance of cruising the high seas with a new 12-book series....

MEDITERRANEAN NIGHTS

Coming in July 2007...

SCENT OF A WOMAN

by

Joanne Rock

When Danielle Chevalier is invited to an exclusive conference aboard *Alexandra's Dream*, she knows it will mean good things for her struggling fragrance company. But her dreams get a setback when she meets Adam Burns, a representative from a large American conglomerate.

Danielle is charmed by the brusque American—until she finds out he means to compete with her bid for the opportunity that will save her family business!

Silhouette®

Romantic
SUSPENSE

**Sparked by Danger,
Fueled by Passion.**

Mission: Impassioned

A brand-new miniseries begins with

My Spy

By *USA TODAY* bestselling author

Marie Ferrarella

She had to trust him with her life....
It was the most daring mission of Joshua Lazlo's
career: rescuing the prime minister of England's
daughter from a gang of cold-blooded kidnappers.
But nothing prepared the shadowy secret agent
for a fiery woman whose touch ignited something
far more dangerous.

My Spy

#1472

Available July 2007 wherever you buy books!

nocturne™

**DON'T MISS THE RIVETING CONCLUSION
TO THE RAINTREE TRILOGY**

RAINTREE: SANCTUARY

by *New York Times* bestselling author

BEVERLY
BARTON

Mercy, guardian of the Raintree
homeplace, takes a stand against
the Ansara wizards to battle for
the Clan's future.

*On sale July,
wherever books are sold.*

SNRT2

REQUEST YOUR FREE BOOKS!

2 FREE NOVELS PLUS 2 FREE GIFTS!

Silhouette *Desire*®

Passionate, Powerful, Provocative!

YES! Please send me 2 FREE Silhouette Desire® novels and my 2 FREE gifts. After receiving them, if I don't wish to receive any more books, I can return the shipping statement marked "cancel." If I don't cancel, I will receive 6 brand-new novels every month and be billed just $3.80 per book in the U.S., or $4.47 per book in Canada, plus 25¢ shipping and handling per book and applicable taxes, if any*. That's a savings of almost 15% off the cover price! I understand that accepting the 2 free books and gifts places me under no obligation to buy anything. I can always return a shipment and cancel at any time. Even if I never buy another book from Silhouette, the two free books and gifts are mine to keep forever.

225 SDN EEXJ 326 SDN EEXU

Name	(PLEASE PRINT)	
Address		Apt.
City	State/Prov.	Zip/Postal Code

Signature (if under 18, a parent or guardian must sign)

Mail to the **Silhouette Reader Service**™:
IN U.S.A.: P.O. Box 1867, Buffalo, NY 14240-1867
IN CANADA: P.O. Box 609, Fort Erie, Ontario L2A 5X3

Not valid to current Silhouette Desire subscribers.

Want to try two free books from another line?
Call 1-800-873-8635 or visit www.morefreebooks.com.

* Terms and prices subject to change without notice. NY residents add applicable sales tax. Canadian residents will be charged applicable provincial taxes and GST. This offer is limited to one order per household. All orders subject to approval. Credit or debit balances in a customer's account(s) may be offset by any other outstanding balance owed by or to the customer. Please allow 4 to 6 weeks for delivery.

Your Privacy: Silhouette is committed to protecting your privacy. Our Privacy Policy is available online at www.eHarlequin.com or upon request from the Reader Service. From time to time we make our lists of customers available to reputable firms who may have a product or service of interest to you. If you would prefer we not share your name and address, please check here. ☐

HARLEQUIN *Presents*

THE ROYAL HOUSE OF NIROLI

Always passionate, always proud.

**The richest royal family in the world—
a family united by blood and passion,
torn apart by deceit and desire.**

Step into the glamorous, enticing world of the
Nirolian Royal Family. As the king ails he must find an
heir…each month an exciting new installment follows
the epic search for the true Nirolian king. Eight heirs,
eight romances, eight fantastic stories!

It's time for playboy prince Marco Fierezza to
claim his rightful place…on the throne of Niroli!
Emily loves Marco, but she has no idea he's a royal
prince! What will this king-in-waiting do when he
discovers his mistress is pregnant?

THE FUTURE KING'S PREGNANT MISTRESS

by Penny Jordan

(#2643)

On sale July 2007.

www.eHarlequin.com   HP12643

COMING NEXT MONTH

#1807 THE CEO'S SCANDALOUS AFFAIR—
Roxanne St. Claire
Dynasties: The Garrisons
He needed her for just one night—but the repercussions of their
sensual evening could last a lifetime!

#1808 HIGH-SOCIETY MISTRESS—Katherine Garbera
The Mistresses
He will stop at nothing to take over his business rival's
company…including bedding his enemy's daughter and making
her his mistress.

#1809 MARRIED TO HIS BUSINESS—Elizabeth Bevarly
Millionaire of the Month
To get his assistant back this CEO plans to woo and seduce her.
But he isn't prepared when she ups the stakes on *his* game.

#1810 THE PRINCE'S ULTIMATE DECEPTION—
Emilie Rose
Monte Carlo Affairs
It was a carefree vacation romance. Until she discovers she's
having an affair with a prince in disguise.

#1811 ROSSELLINI'S REVENGE AFFAIR—
Yvonne Lindsay
He blamed her for his family's misery and sought revenge in a
most passionate way!

#1812 THE BOSS'S DEMAND—Jennifer Lewis
She was pregnant with the boss's baby—but wanted more than
just the convenient marriage he was offering.